SURVIVING

SURVIVING

edited by
Michael Blackburn

SUNK ISLAND PUBLISHING

LINCOLN

SURVIVING is issue 7 of *Sunk Island Review*
published by Sunk Island Publishing 1993.
Copyright © this collection, Sunk Island Publishing 1993
Copyright © the authors 1993

EDITOR Michael Blackburn
PRODUCTION John Wardle
COVER DESIGN Geoffrey Mark Matthews
EDITORIAL ASSISTANT Sylvia Blackburn

The financial assistance
of Eastern Arts Board
is gratefully acknowledged.

ISSN 0955-9647
ISBN 1 874778 15 9

All submissions (including those from literary agents)
should be accompanied by stamped addressed envelopes
or International Reply Coupons, otherwise they will
not be considered.

SUNK ISLAND PUBLISHING
P.O. Box 74
Lincoln LN1 1QG
England

CONTENTS

PHILIP SIDNEY JENNINGS.
    Moving On   7
PETER RYDE.
    Survivors   17
ANNIE WRIGHT.
    Not Making It   36
MATTHEW CALEY.
    Canadian Bouywaa   38
WANG JIAXIN. *Translated by John Cayley*
    Scorpion   41
    Change   42
    Empty Valley   44
    Stairway   45
    Homeland   46
JUDI BENSON.
    Why England?   47
    Whya Not East Ham?   48
STEPHEN GREGORY.
    The City of Eternal Youth   52
JOSÉ HIERRO. *Translated by Louis Bourne*
    Hallucination of America   62
ROBERTO JUARROZ. *Translated by Louis Bourne*
    Vertical Poetry 1   66
    Vertical Poetry 2   67
MIKE JENKINS.
    No Perfection   68
JANET FISHER.
    Freesias   70
FRANS POINTL. *Translated by James Brockway*
    The Survivors   71
NICHOLAS ROYLE.
    Shades of Monk   82

CONTRIBUTORS   95

HALLOWED GROUND

by *Robert Edric*

Summer, 1945, and the small German town of Waldsdorf has become the centre for thousands of refugees, deserters and displaced persons. Allied troops arrive – together with their Intelligence Officers – producing a volatile atmosphere.

Waldsdorf has hardly been touched by the war, but there is growing unrest and resentment at the uncertainties of peace. The town hides at its core a secret by which all its inhabitants know they must be judged – and ultimately condemned. Once uncovered, it is a secret that sets in motion an unstoppable trail of violence in which the townsfolk themselves seek their final redemption.

A timely novel for our disturbing age, from the prize-winning author of *In the Day of the American Museum* ('powerful writing' – *The Times*) and *The Broken Lands* ('Elemental, wonderful and compelling' – *City Limits*).

Publication launch at Ilkley Literature Festival, 18th June.

Retail price £6.99. Subscribers to *Sunk Island Review* may buy their copies at £5.99, post-free. Cheques/P.O.s should be made payable to Sunk Island Publishing.

Paperback   120pp   ISBN 1 874778 05 1

SUNK ISLAND PUBLISHING
P.O. Box 74, Lincoln LN1 1QG

MOVING ON

Philip Sidney Jennings

My wife and son are in France so I sit in our little suburban garden thinking about them and wondering who my new neighbours are. I can hear them rummaging about and I can't stop worrying the three or four wiry hairs that curl out of one nostril. My sun-glasses slide down my sweaty nose and although it's a futile activity to push them up, I do so, again and again. The wings of my book flutter from time to time. It's my birthday and as there's a postal strike and engineers have inadvertently severed the local telephone cable I can only remind myself that once more I am a year older. A pity really, these birthdays and numbers: nothing more than signposts to senility and death, small wonder so many people celebrate with a large dose of oblivion. I drop my deck-chair another notch, admire the nut tan my belly has acquired this summer and enter the gates of positive thinking.

This sunny September afternoon is a gift. The faintest breeze kisses my face and rustles the newspaper on the grass, only occasionally does it awake the memory of pawed-over cat shit deposited by my other neighbours' beasts who prefer my little garden to their own. Of course I've told the two witches about their cats but they just flash their eyes and threaten me with spells. I was always worried my son might step in the shit or worse.

To my novel then. I pick it up and look across the garden and see immediately my new neighbour's fat arse through the gaps in the fence. She's wearing frayed shorts which part an uncompromising black pubic thatch and she's watering an uncertain cheese-plant and talking to it.

'There you are Frederick. You're going to like it here. Have a drink, you'll feel much better. You look a bit dowdy. Don't be dowdy.'

She turns abruptly, walks to the fence and extends her hand plus arm towards me:

'Hello, I'm Wendy. We've just moved in.'

She has short dark hair, a definite nose and a build to match her arse in comparative geometry.

'Hang on,' I say, 'don't let your arm drop off.'

I struggle out of the plastic sweat of the deck-chair and finally grasp her.

'Rudolph, how's it going?'

She points at the house,

'It's all there. Martin's levering open crates and being macho.'

'Someone's got to.'

'He's going out to buy a sledgehammer. We want to make a garden, get rid of all this concrete.'

I see an opportunity to be positive and don't let it go by.

'You won't regret it. The soil here is wonderful. I've grown courgettes, leaks, carrots, you name it. If it weren't for the slugs and cats you could eat the earth.'

She smiles happily at her entertaining neighbour so I go on to say that I read until four in the morning, slept until one and didn't hear the old neighbours move out and them move in. I can tell she's pleased with me so I go on a bit more and say I hope they'll be happy here and my wife and son are in France and if they need tea-bags I have at least two hundred and are they O.K. for milk because I've got lots and the milkman delivers six days a week and he's a good bloke and I'm forty-three years old today and what a beautiful day it is and I remember when I moved in, how the weather was so cold and my son was so small, a baby.

'You're a Virgo,' Wendy says, 'that's a good sign. I'm Taurus.'

'That's a good sign too,' I say, 'there's nothing wrong with being a Taurus, quite the opposite …'

Martin has been listening or just happens to come out then. We shake hands across the fence. He's wearing old-style national-health glasses, long black shorts and door-step trainers. His hair everywhere is ginger. He's cooler than Wendy, less forthright and in his eyes there's something like a confident awareness. I imagine Wendy and three pints of real ale would bring him wholely alive. Before I can launch in to tell him about the neighbourhood he points out a couple of things.

'I see you're growing Jerusalem artichokes, don't see them very often. Very lush. Your garden's just a bit higher than ours.'

'My wife planted those. She calls them Canada or something like that. I never noticed the slope of the gardens before, never thought about it.'

He nods as though to say he notices lots of things and gestures at the concrete.

'I'm getting a hammer. We'll be a bit noisy for a while. If you need anything broken up?'

I hate being disturbed with noise but I don't say that. I point at a mighty deformity of concrete which came free with the house.

'Maybe that, I've been meaning to get rid of it.'

'No problem. I may hire a drill.'

I shudder as though I'm already on the end of the drill.

'I didn't know you could hire them.'

'Oh you can hire anything,' he informs me.

'We're getting a skip if you want to get rid of anything,' Wendy adds and I say,

'A big dead telly. Been meaning to get rid of that.'

'No problem.'

They want to leave then and hire the things but I mention the Indian Summer and France and the soil and tea-bags and my birthday. They listen politely, don't wish me a happy birthday and tear themselves away with busy smiles.

'Good luck,' I say kindly and stick my back into the deck-chair like a stamp on an envelope.

'Thanks,' Martin says, 'I'm going to make a herb garden in the back.'

They leave and I'm left with a ridiculous tendril of jealousy sprouting out of my head. After a while a thought comes into my head: if they get rid of the concrete and have grass and earth they'll also have their share of cat deposits. I then stop feeling oddly envious and go to the kitchen for food, bung it all on a tray: yoghurt, apple, biscuits, cheese, and get back to my chair and the sunshine. I eat the pulpy muck, tell myself I'm not human and it's good for me and think about my wife's savoury cooking. I certainly miss it. I'm a good cook but why make something delicious if there's no-one to share the deliciousness with?

And so to the novel. All novels are about misfits and *Jane Eyre* is no exception. I read a page, two pages, whack a wasp, turn the page, forget the process and realize after a while I've read quite a lot and the sun is losing its power, moving on elsewhere for somebody else.

A movement next door, not the witches, but Martin and Wendy, they're back. I hear their back door open and stare down at my book without reading and unsure of suburban ethics: do you pretend in the name of privacy that people separated from you by a few feet and a fence aren't really there? I've never been sure about that. I decide not to speak to them unless they speak to me first. The forsythia tree my wife cultivated gives some privacy and in fact it's behind the tree that Martin sets up a tressle table and Wendy brings some dishes to it. They sit outside and talk and eat. I hide behind my glasses and book and try to hear what they are saying but it's not easy as they've lowered their voices and they are busy eaters,

'The brass bed is up at least…we could make a room under the roof, a window…I'm painting over my wall-paper…I'm not in the front room …'

The last bit I find interesting because that means they're not married and have separate plans in the same small house. My wife and I always agree about house alterations, the problem is getting the money to effect them. Martin says,

'Those spring onions were powerful.'

Wendy says

'I love the market,' and I hear in her voice, though my wife would probably say I was 'being cynical', an eye for a bargain, Mother Nature and the love of a simple idyllic peasant way of life. I shake my head and really want to tell her that she'd do better to buy her vegetables and fruit from the supermarket, that way it's your own fault if you go home with a dodgy pear.

'Rudolph.'

Wendy is beaming and I get the impression she may have fallen in love with me. I wriggle upright in the chair.

'Hello Wendy.'

'We don't want to be anti-social but is it O.K. if Martin breaks up some concrete now?'

Martin appear with a slim smile and a great big hammer. I can hardly tell them it's not O.K. and I must content myself with the fact that they asked me first. I roll into the expected role.

'Of course, go ahead,' I say and wonder if they've asked the Pakistani family that live on their other side. Not my business anyway.

Thunk! I shudder and realize that I won't be able to read in the garden with that noise. Wendy, it seems, feels like a chat.

'Do you like dancing Rudolph?'

This is an odd question to ask someone like me and I feel a bit intimidated. Still I'm reluctant to say I prefer reading and appear stodgy.

'Er, sometimes I do, yes.'

I trail away trying to remember if my wife and I have ever been dancing together. Probably not, but then with a small boy you can't always do what you feel like.

Wendy tells me about her friend Devona who's opening a West-Indian night club in Stoke Newington.

'She's got the licence now. Lot of hassle but she's got it. You'll meet her. She's such a laugh and she's got bags of energy.'

My face contracts to a poker. I'm always wary of happy people, perhaps the reverse is true. Poor Devona, I don't want to meet her, I feel intimidated already.

'Just as I thought. Rubble.'

As they say in books:Martin mops his brow. Wendy shoots him a concerned look, secretly glad he's being macho I suppose. I also shoot Martin a weary sympathetic look and expect him to down tool and go for a deck-chair. But no, he's made of finer stuff. He raises his hammer on high,

'I'll find the earth eventually.'

Thunk! Shudder. I know he will.

'Anyway Rudolph,' Wendy speaks through a smile (quite difficult),

'You must come round for a drink later, yes?'

A drink. A strange question to ask a reindeer? hesitate though. Even without Devona they may possibly be too happy for me. But then again the sun is plummeting past the yard-arm and this new couple still excite me. The previous couple though only in their thirties, were literally deaf if you used words or phrases beyond their range. Still we got on well together providing the conversation didn't last for more than ten minutes.

I give Wendy a firm positive look,

'Fine. Right. What time?'

'Any time you like.'

She beams. She is a beamer. I glance at my watch. I need to run from the hammer and lie on the bed and see if I'm depressed or not. I may well be all right.

'I'll ring your bell at seven,' I say,

'Fine.'

Everything is fine. Wendy slopes off. Martin raises his weapon. I go inside and up to my bed, lie down and think about my life, my wife, myself, my handsome little son. I can see his little shining face and I wrap my arms around the pillow.

I start. I was just chasing a marvellous revelation but I've woke myself up to hold and analyse it. And now...it's gone. Ten to seven sadness. The doorbell pierces. Who can that be? But I know.

Wendy stands at the door and sips a tall can of real-ish ale.

'You coming round then Rudolph?'

We've known each other only a matter of hours and she doubts me already?

'Mmm, want to come in a minute.'

'Sure.'

I lead her into the front room. Her eyes rove until they settle in a corner.

'That's really whacky!'

In the corner is a small black and white telly on a chair and nothing else.

'What's whacky?'

'That chair.'

The chair is wooden and falling to pieces. It's no good for sitting on. I really can't remember where it comes from.

'Someone told me they're called Captain's Chair.'

'Really whacky.'

It's probably not a bad thing to be a bit whacky and I follow Wendy who drifts into the dining room dominated by a mammoth fridge, no comment there, so she's into the tiny kitchen and out again quite quickly to tap on the wall which divides dining room and kitchen. She seems at home so I just listen to her tapping. She turns to me,

'Rudolph, knock this wall down, it's not brick, no problem, hey presto, you have a large kitchen-diner.'

I drop into a chair.

'You wouldn't like to do it for me, would you?'

'Yeah, I'll give you hand.'

She gives the plaster another whack and I get the impression she's about to start on the job.

'There's probably gas pipes in there.'

'They can be moved around.'

I trail after her to the foot of the stairs. Here she hesitates, I suppose realizing that upstairs is more intimate and demands an invitation.

'Up you go,' I say and up she goes.

I stomp after her. The front room is a place of abandoned hobbies: wood-carving, painting, foot-ball pools coupons, books, newspapers, envelopes, curriculum vitaes, children's toys. She makes a sound of vague approval but I am glad to leave this room and enter the bed-room where the sheets and covers descend in waves and dead snotty tissues punctuate the floor. Quickly then into the boy's little room full of posters, bears, more toys, a pram, confusion.

'Nice,' she says through a belch over the top of her can and reminds me it's time for a drink. I wonder if there's anything I need to do before going next door but it doesn't seem so: I follow her out of my house and into theirs.

I sit down on a brown leather sofa opposite a too loud stereo and note that they already have a kitchen diner. Foolishly I tell myself they've made that conversion in the few hours they've been here. Bob Dylan sings about suburban nirvana, cardboard boxes erupt and the frowning face of Nelson Mandela stares down at me from a poster on the wall. Certainly they've put that poster up since they've moved in and it wasn't left by my previous neighbour who complained in veiled tones about the smell of curry and fried onions at breakfast time.

Martin comes in hot and sweaty and polite, a man who's earned a drink.

'Lager or beer Rudolph?'

'I don't know. Anything. Beer.'

'Right, no problem. Mind if I turn it down a bit Wendy?'

She appreciates his concern and gestures liberally. Bob fades and I get a can which I quickly unzip. We sit together drinking through the key-hole of the can. They don't offer a glass and I don't ask for one. Wendy lights up a cigarette so I do the same and she seems pleased and aims an ash-tray at me.

'Martin used to smoke, more than me, he gave it up they don't like it at his job anyway, Martin's a barrister.'

Immediately I feel jealous and wish I were a barrister but I find a crooked smile and say,

'How fresh and young you look for a barrister.' He smiles carefully behind his cheap glasses,

'I always knew what I wanted to do. Incidentally I'm going to set up a law centre in the area. There isn't one is there?'

'Don't think so.'

'We'll do it together,' Wendy says, 'I'm nearly a solicitor now. We'll work for Greenpeace, anti-racist movement, that sort of thing. It's going to be fun.'

I inhale deeply, blow a plume of smoke and hide Nelson in a cloud, but he shouldn't worry, not with Wendy and Martin on his case.

Then Wendy asks me.

'What do you do yourself Rudolph?'

My face moves here and there but eventually settles on to some familiar ledges. I speak to the best of my ability without emotion.

'I'm a supply teacher but the borough's run out of money so they say, so there's no work. I've got a couple of hundred quid …'

Despite myself I trail away and dissolve into a triangular silence which Wendy quickly breaks much like my wife,

'You can go to another borough surely?'

I drain my can. Sterling Martin is swiftly on his feet. He moves without envy or advice.

'Let's have another beer.'

'You've got a good man there,' I say and spread my sensual lips and reveal my near-perfect teeth.

'Oh Martin's all right.'

She dismisses him with a belch and stares at me. I feel I ought to say something. This comes out,

'We old hippies with English degrees are an abomination to the nation. I get the feeling I'm supposed to be a computer now, something like that.'

Oddly they both like that as though I've said something subversive to the state. Martin says as we pull our key-holes,

'We're taking a cruise as soon as Wendy's qualified.'

'What about the law centre?' I ask.

'That may have to wait.'

I exchange looks with Nelson. His frown doesn't change.

Suddenly Wendy gets up and puts an envelope and a bottle wrapped in happy-birthday paper next to me on the sofa.

'Happy birthday Rudolph,' they say. Immediately I am confused and embarrassed. I find a half bottle of classy wine and a card that reads,

'We hope neighbours will be friends.' Both have written love. Martin has indicated two kisses, Wendy three. What shall I do? Arise from the sofa and stick my tongue down their throats?

'That's very sweet of you,' I say and keep my eyes on my beer as I'm embarrassed more by their cliche than their gift.

'Good. We thought you were alone.'

'No problem. Don't mention it.'

After that, Wendy belches and talks about feminism, Martin turns up Bob, who seems to have more energy than all of us and I tilt my can and feel very uncomfortable. It's time I went back to my bed to see how I feel. Martin suggests another beer so I say,

'Well, thanks, O.K. but the last one, I should get back.'

They nod with good understanding and I wonder what they will say about me when I've gone. I attack the new beer quite fiercely. I want to get away now. I don't want to reveal anything more about myself. I don't want anything like a 'meaningful discussion'. It occurs to me they must think I'm boring, sitting there, saying nothing. Wendy starts singing and Martin has adopted a far-away relaxed pose. Suddenly I'm saved by the phone ringing in my house. I leap up.

'The phone! It's been off. It's on. Mended. I must catch that. Could be France for me.'

I'm on the move, rushing politely.

'Don't forget your bottle and card.'

I flee with smiles and thanks. Keys out, twist, into the house, find the phone on the stairs, dive, and the wretched thing stops ringing. I pick it up but of course, it's dead.

A dead feeling enters me. I'm not hungry or thirsty but I finish my can and open the little bottle of wine and bring out a brick of cheese and a pack of boring biscuits. It's dark and starless outside. I wander from room to room chomping and cursing crumbs. I don't know which room to be in but know I will soon beach myself on the sofa in front of the television. The little bottle of wine is soon gone and its classy label sleeps in the garbage with all the other polythene and paper boasts. I open my familiar two pound bottle of Côte de Whatever, sigh twice, stretch out and let the T.V. become my head. The news tells me a little boy has gone missing and I squirm with pain knowing that even as I lie on the sofa that boy may be moving to his death in the throes of inconceivable pain.

The phone goes, I jump and move fast to it. I clear my head and present a voice,

'Yes, hello.'

As usual her voice is slow and level.

'Hello Rudolph, happy birthday to you.'

Sophie, thanks, how are you, all right, how's the boy?

'Oh, we're all right, he's fine, he's been playing with the rabbits all day.'

Relief spreads through me but the line is bad and I feel a bit sick. I blurt things out, about the phone and the post and work, and the neighbours. I can see her face hardly changing expression.

'Are you drunk?'

'No, no. Had a few drinks with the new neighbours.'
'They sound like yuppies.'
'Well I don't know.'
'Still, at least they're doing things.'

I know what she means: I'm not. We're falling into familiar grooves. The phone is going funny.

'I've been offered a job…wondering whether to take it…can you hear me Rudolph?'

She's talking about money and her mother looking after the boy and how difficult it is in England. In a micro-second of fantastic rage I want to smash up the physical world around me. I don't know what to say. Next door I can hear Martin and Wendy playing the Beatles.

'When will I see you?' I shout into the phone.
'Call you during the week… it's a bad line.'

She hangs up and I feel relieved and frustrated and inadequate. I don't know what to do.

So I do what I always do at this time. I stumble drunkenly from the front room to the dining room, into the kitchen, into the bathroom. I mount the scales. My weight has not changed. I can still weigh myself. Nineteen and a half stone. I tell myself there's nothing I can do about Sophie and the boy and work yet. Not tonight anyway. Tomorrow can be different.

I'll get up early, fresh and bright. I'll find a job in another borough. I'll jog and lose weight. I'll telephone Sophie and tell her life is possible here and how much I miss the little boy. I'll get things together. No-one will lack anything. We'll be happy just like Jane Eyre was eventually. It'll be a struggle but we'll be all right. I feel better for these positive thoughts and go back to the sofa for a lie-down…But next door Martin is drilling holes in the wall. Poor wall. I wish he'd stop. His activity tires me. It sounds so meaningless. Just because you move doesn't mean you've got to be so busy. I wonder when I'll see Sophie and my boy again. I want to collapse but I've already collapsed on the sofa. Then I remember how positive I'm going to be in the morning and I can't help but feel much better.

SURVIVORS

Peter Ryde

1.

The new pound coins played a strange trick on me. Not long after they came out, I bought a quid's worth of cigarettes with a tenner. The man on the till held out nine of the bright gold coins in his cupped hands and dropped them with a flourish onto the polished wooden counter in front of me.

For a split second, I was a kid again, playing Pontoon with Major Croxley.

He used to take an interest. His 'warphanage'. God knows how he got away with it, except that in those days people had eyes and saw not.

The first step was a preliminary inspection. Newcomers were sent up to the house in groups for Sunday lunch. He was said to mark you out of ten and write down particulars in a card index. Anyone showing appropriate potential would be invited back on subsequent occasions.

He was very particular about the way you dressed. White shirts were obligatory – it was the only time we ever got out of the institutional blue – and any boy who turned up wearing a snake-buckle belt was sent back to change it. Punctuality was equally important. More than a minute late or early, and you were given a lecture right there on the doorstep about how to behave like a gentleman.

The first time I went, I was with Roy and Andy. Andy I liked. Roy I didn't. The truth is, I was afraid of him. Whatever I said or did, he could put me down with a scornful lift of his eyebrow, and I'd know he was right. He'd been to America; and he could strip down a motor mower and put it together again without any bits left over. The word was that his father had been a Brigadier; only in that case, you wouldn't have thought that Roy would have been in care.

We stood by the hedge just round the corner from the gate, waiting to hear the church clock strike twelve; then we walked up the path in a line and Roy rang the bell. Ten or fifteen seconds later, there was a blurred movement behind the Flemish glass. Major Croxley opened the door and stood for a moment, looking down at us. He was lean and tall, with a starched collar and vigorous bushy eyebrows. You could imagine him having a native bearer flogged to death.

'Come in, and tell me your names,' he said.

Roy stepped into the hall and shook hands. Of course, he would know to do this. 'Good Morning, sir. I'm Roy, this is Andy. And that's Jamie.'

'Haven't the others got tongues in their heads?' said the Major, and Roy blushed.

I was last into the house. For a moment or two, I saw no prospect of getting beyond the doormat. The Major harpooned me to the spot with a fierce glance, as though I was some kind of degenerate. He smelt of soap and moral values.

'How old are you?'

'Thirteen.'

'Then you're too old for a little boy's name. I shall call you James.' Suddenly, he gave me a broad wink and propelled me towards the others, his hand pressing firmly against my back.

To start with, we sat in his study. There were books and papers all over the room; in the far corner was a roll-top desk with a typewriter and a pile of manuscript. He wrote learned books about certain obscure aspects of military history.

'Sherry,' he announced. 'Apologies in advance. Can't get decent stuff any more. Meths dyed with gravy browning, I shouldn't wonder. Typical of the wogs.'

He handed round the glasses. 'Don't suppose they give you much of this down the road, eh? Tea with a good dollop of bromide, if I know anything, and all hands on deck, what? Still, I dare say you're better off than poor old Oliver Twist.'

Roy was doing his best not to giggle. After an experimental sip I decided that sherry was horrible and I would very much rather be somewhere else. Only Andy was unperturbed; but nothing ever seemed to bother him. I suppose it came from knowing there wasn't a lot else the world could do to him.

For the next fifteen minutes, I sat in a state of semi-catatonia whilst Roy and the Major talked man-to-man about things I'd never heard of. I wished I could think of anything at all to say.

'You're very silent, James.'

I shrugged, and stared at my feet.

'Well now. Tell me about yourself. What are you good at? What's your favourite sport?'

'Swimming, I suppose.'

'Swimming?' His tiny flicker of interest dwindled into extinction. 'Splendid. Jolly good. Good.'

At precisely one o'clock, we moved into the dining room. The stiff white tablecloth, reaching almost to the floor, was laid with cut glass and gigantic silver cutlery; there was a bowl of flowers in the centre, and candles burning.

The Major steered us to our places and began slicing into the crust of a large oval pie, serving the portions with elegant efficiency. While we were awkwardly helping ourselves to vegetables from delicately patterned china dishes, he filled our tumblers with Fruit Cup from a tall glass jug with a silver rim. There were lumps of fruit floating about in it, which had to be held back with a special little strainer.

Roy was on the Major's left, Andy on his right. My own position, at the foot of the table, was a mixed blessing. I was out of his reach, but on the other hand I was exposed to his direct line of vision. After struggling for several minutes with the enormous knife and fork I became aware that he was continually staring at me and then glancing away in irritation. I slid lower in my chair, and hoped the candles would hide me.

Finally, exasperated beyond endurance, he said, 'James, dear boy, I really don't care to see you holding your knife and fork in that vulgar fashion. Do try to be more civilised, there's a good chap.'

I gazed round blankly at the others, wondering what I was doing wrong. I shifted my grip slightly, and tried to copy Roy; but this found no favour and I spent the remainder of the meal in unredeemed damnation, scarcely daring to eat.

Afterwards we sat in the study again, and drank pungent oily coffee out of tiny cups. Taking advantage of the Major's temporary absence, I ventured a carefully restrained grimace. 'He doesn't make very good coffee.'

Roy snapped impatiently, 'It's Turkish. It's meant to be like that.'

When the Major returned they started talking knowledgeably about shot-guns and what would happen if you ate game and accidentally swallowed a pellet.

'Why don't they take the pellets out?' I said.

'Can't always find 'em.' He smiled distantly. 'Listen. I'll tell you something that happened once. Man standing right next to me had a mis-fire; peppered me all over, silly beggar. Doctors took out all they could find, but later on I kept coming across more. Wouldn't take 'em out, though. Not worth the trouble. No danger, apparently.'

'You mean they're still there?' said Roy, taken aback.

'Yes. And I've got ten bob that says you can't find one of 'em in sixty seconds flat. Come on. Give it a try.'

We glanced at one another uneasily.

'Come on, Roy. You first. I'll give you a clue. Above the waist, right hand side. I'll just slip my jacket off; make it a bit easier.'

Roy slid his hands cautiously along the Major's arm and down his back without finding anything.

'Time's running out,' said the Major, staring intently at his watch. Roy brought his hands round onto the Major's chest, and I saw his fingertips hover doubtfully over a spot just below the ribs. He pressed a little harder, and then said confidently, 'There, I think.'

The Major beamed at him in delight. 'Splendid. Good lad. Two seconds to spare, what?' He suddenly produced a ten shilling note, folded it carefully in four, and pushed it well down into Roy's trouser pocket. He seemed anxious to make sure it was safely in.

'Thank you very much, sir,' said Roy, and went back to his place looking pleased with himself.

'Now Andrew,' said the Major. 'Above the waist, left hand side.'

Andy didn't move. For three or four seconds they stared at each other; then Andy slowly stood up and crossed the room to where the Major was sitting. Keeping as far away as possible, he ran his fingers perfunctorily over the Major's arm, looking as if he wished he was wearing rubber gloves. After a few seconds, he pressed one finger against the soft hollow of the Major's elbow, and then stood well back.

The Major was trying not to look disappointed. 'Well done.' He held out another ten bob note. Andy stood completely still for a few moments, then slowly reached out and took it. Soon afterwards, when the Major's back was turned, he slipped the note into the narrow space under the carriage clock on the mantelpiece. It seemed rather a waste. Ten bob was money.

The Major sought out my eyes and sent me a genial smile. 'There's still one left, James. But yours'll have to be below the waist.'

For one dreadful moment, I thought he might be going to take his trousers off. He motioned me to kneel down on the floor in front of him. Very gingerly, I started to explore his ankles, and then slid a hand up the back of each leg. His calf muscles felt hard and knobbly.

'Try a bit higher.'

I tried his knees.

'Further up, James. Time's running out.'

I felt hot and slightly dizzy. My arms were paralysed. 'It's no good. I can't find it.'

'Tell you what. You didn't have any clues about left or right, so we'll give you an extension. Twenty seconds extra. Don't give up the ship.'

I moved my hands until they rested just above his knees. My left index finger seemed to be touching a small bump. Thankfully, I made a feeble pretence of testing this. 'Is that it?' I said at last.

'Time's up,' said the Major. 'Sorry, old boy. All you've found is a varicose vein. Bad luck. Never mind.'

As I scuttled back to my chair, my face was burning like the top of a Christmas pudding. I could sense that Roy was looking at me in derision. 'God, you're pathetic,' he said, half under his breath.

By this time we were deemed to have digested our dinner, so the Major announced that we should now go outside and play Bumblepuppy. 'Leave your coats in here. As a matter of fact, why not slip your shirts off as well? You'll be much too hot otherwise.'

I was glad of the chance. The best thing about Sunday clothes was taking them off. Roy pulled his shirt off too, but Andy kept his on. I wasn't surprised. he hated people asking about his scars.

Bumblepuppy was a novelty to all three of us, being, I suppose, at least a generation out of date already; in later life, I only ever met two other people who had even heard of it. Two players stand one each side of a vertical post, about eight feet high, which has a six foot rope fastened to the top of it. On the free end of the rope is a net with a tennis ball in it. By hitting the ball with rackets, each player tries to wind the rope round the pole, one clockwise, one anticlockwise. It's the sort of game that intrigues you for ten minutes; then it suddenly dawns on you that it's the most futile occupation anyone could think of.

'Andrew and James can start,' said the Major. 'Roy and I will criticise.'

Andy played with detached efficiency, and I with my usual incompetence. Once or twice, he hit the ball rather viciously; it swung out on the end of the rope, and I had to leap backwards suddenly to get out of the way. The second time it happened, I cannonned straight into the Major, who felt it necessary to grip me tightly to stop me falling. 'Steady the Buffs,' he commented. 'Anyway, I think it's Roy's turn now.'

Roy took the racket and started to play. Meanwhile, as we watched, the Major held me close in front of him, his arms draped gently across my chest. After a time, he placed his hands firmly on to my shoulders and pushed me about a foot away from him, as if he were shifting furniture. I felt him run his thumb all the way along my spine from the nape of my neck right down into the waistband of my trousers.

'My dear boy,' he said, suddenly sounding very concerned. 'You stand extremely badly. You'll do yourself an injury if you slouch like that. I think we'll probably need to do some work on you.'

My protests were brushed aside. He would, he announced, be getting in touch.

2.

'But Jamie,' said Mrs Urquhart, whose name I didn't learn to spell till later, 'it's very kind of the Major to take the trouble. He knows about these things. He'll be able to show you some exercises to help improve your posture.'

On balance, I should have preferred to grow up as a hunchback. But having broken a window that very morning I was an undischarged debtor and in no position to resist, especially as the ball, like most of our games equipment, our radiogram, and heaven knows what else, had been donated by the Major. It seemed there was nothing for it but to pay him a call at half past two the following Sunday, as instructed.

The morning before my visit, out on the hillside, Andy was sharing his last cigarette with me. He was a comfortable person to be with; no manoeuvring, no scoring of points. I'd felt completely safe with him from the first day we met. He liked to wrestle me, and sometimes he took it a bit further; but I didn't mind. It seemed companionable, uncomplicated.

'You'll have to watch it with the Major, Jamie,' he said.

'Yeah. But it's funny, though. I thought it was Roy he fancied.'

I handed the butt back. With luck, Andy could squeeze a last drag before he chucked it.

'Certainly looked that way. Smokescreen, perhaps. Or maybe he hasn't thought of another excuse yet. Both of you can't have sagging spines.'

'There's nothing the matter with my spine.'

'How can you tell?'

'No one's said anything before.'

'Let's have a look.'

I pulled my shirt over my head and leant forward. The summer sun felt warm on my skin as Andy's fingers explored my vertebrae.

'Seems O.K. to me. Stand up a minute, though.'

I loosened my belt to let him feel the small of my back. He gave a doubtful little grunt. 'Maybe it does go in a bit. Just a little.'

'Where?' I said, in disbelief.

He guided my hand to the place.

'What about yours?' I asked. 'Its probably just the same.'

He slipped his shirt off to let me look. I'd seen his scars dozen of times, but even so I couldn't help catching my breath. He'd been in Singapore when the Japs got in. One day, they tied him up and beat him in front of his parents to make his father talk. A week later, he'd seen them both being hacked to pieces. It wasn't a thing he cared to speak about, but he mentioned it to me once in the middle of the night, when the two of us were lying awake, admitting things.

I pressed my fingers lightly against the base of his spine. 'There's no difference,' I said.

He shrugged. 'Croxley's shooting a line, then.'

'I know. But what can I do?'

'Eat beans. If the worst comes to the worst, fart in his face.'

I could have done with some company as I walked up the Major's front path the following afternoon. Even Roy would have been better than nothing. To fill in time after I'd rung the bell, I started repeating the alphabet under my breath, a trick I'd learned in the Blitz, and still found useful whenever I was afraid.

'Ah. James.'

The Major took me into the study and sat down at his desk.

'Right. Let's have a good look at you. Everything off.'

I hesitated.

'Come on, boy. I haven't got all day.'

I took all my clothes off and stood as far away from him as I could. He watched intently, appraising me with shrewdly critical eyes, like a man buying slaves and hoping to knock twenty per cent off the price. It looked as if I didn't measure up to his expectations.

'Turn round.'

He viewed me from north, south, east and west, and then said curtly, 'Bend over and touch your toes.'

This position, apparently, merited prolonged study. I thought I was there for life. After several minutes, he rose from his chair with a long sigh, positioned himself directly behind me, and started to investigate my central region with the tips of his fingers; they felt dry and slippery, like snakeskin.

'Stand up now.'

I brought my head up too quickly and felt suddenly dizzy. As I put out an arm to steady myself, he caught hold of it, levering me round to face him. 'Your posture is appalling,' he commented. 'Also, I think your pelvis may be slightly tilted. That'll be a long term job. The other we can probably deal with fairly quickly.'

He knelt in front of me, cupping his hands round the back of my thighs. 'I'm going to try and pull you forward. Resist me.'

The next moment, I very nearly fell over on top of him.

'Resist me,' he repeated angrily. 'Brace those legs of yours. I want to feel you hard, boy. Hard. Tighten your muscles. Resist me. Resist me.'

We conducted this grotesque tug of war for about five minutes, his hands moving systematically all over my body. I was jerking this way and that like a daffodil in a squall of wind.

'Good,' he announced at last. 'Now, stand easy. Relax all your muscles. Give yourself to me.'

From the feel of his hands on my body, you'd think I was made out of soft clay and he was trying to squeeze me into a better shape. I tensed up instinctively whenever he touched me, and this irritated him as much as my inadequate resistance earlier on. 'Let me have you. Don't fight it. Let me do what I want. Give. Give. Give.'

Having finally resculptured me to his satisfaction, the Major hurriedly left the room. 'I'll be back directly,' he said, over his shoulder.

'Can I get dressed now?' I called after him.

'No,' he answered sharply from half way up the stairs.

It was a relief to be left on my own. While I was waiting, I crossed over to the window and looked out into the garden. Over on the left, almost out of sight, I could see a flashy two-seater parked on the gravel pathway, its chrome glinting in the sunlight. I didn't remember seeing it before. It must have been in the garage or I should have noticed it when we were playing Bumblepuppy. If it had been anyone else's, I shouldn't have minded a ride in it.

Turning back towards the centre of the room, I noticed the carriage clock on the mantelpiece, and wondered what the time was. Twenty past three. Just as I was looking away again, I remembered Andy's ten bob note. By placing my eye exactly in line with the narrow gap, I could see that it was still there. The little matter of my broken window also came to mind.

'What are you doing, James?'

The Major was standing in the doorway, with a folding camera and what appeared to be a bundle of clothes. Having no pockets, I had nowhere to conceal the note, so I stood there like an idiot, holding the evidence in my hand.

'Where did you get that?'

'It's Andy's. He left it here last Sunday.'

The Major's chin rose slightly as he surveyed me in withering silence. He stepped into the room and put the clothes and the camera down on a chair. Without a word, he held his hand out towards me. When I made no move, he snapped his fingers impatiently. A fuller explanation seemed increasingly impossible the more I thought about it. In the end, I handed him the note, feeling even more acutely aware than before that I was standing in front of him completely naked.

For at least a minute he stared at me with a mixture of anger and contempt. Eventually, pocketing the note, he said, 'I'm very disappointed in you, James. I thought you were a nice boy. I thought you were worth taking some trouble with. I certainly didn't expect to find you were a thief.'

'I'm not.'

'Be silent. I wonder what the Urquharts will have to say when they hear how you repay my hospitality. Not that I take any pleasure in telling tales. In fact, if you'd rather, we can settle the matter between us, here and now.'

'I don't know what you mean.'

He picked up a heavy stick from the corner. 'I'll beat you myself. Hard. Very hard. But then it'll be over, and there'll be no need for either of us to say anything.'

Andy had given me a tip about how to survive a staring match. Instead of looking the other person straight in the eye, you focus on the bridge of their nose. They don't notice the difference, but you can keep it going for ever, even if you're sick with fear. He didn't say whether he'd used it on the Japs, but it certainly worked with the Major.

We faced each other in silence for several minutes. Eventually he turned towards the telephone. 'Very well. You leave me no choice.'

He dialled a number, and waited impassively for a few seconds before putting the receiver down. 'It's engaged,' he said.

He picked up the camera from the chair. 'In the meantime, I shall need some photographs to monitor your progress. There isn't enough light in here: come into the garden.'

I was astounded. 'What, like this?'

'How else?' he snapped, as if to an imbecile.

He posed me in various positions in front of the garden shed and took a selection of pictures. His approach to photography was ponderous and bad-tempered. At one point there was a long pause so that he could change the film. While I was waiting, I glanced over at the sports car. It was half-hidden behind some bushes, so I gradually manoeuvred myself to one side to get a clearer view.

'Ah. You've spotted the MG. Go and look, if you like.'

I wandered over to the car and stood gazing at it with a mixture of wonder and envy. For some reason I felt an irresistible urge to touch it, to caress the smooth bodywork with my fingers, to grip the steering wheel, to feel the leather seat back brushing against my skin. I walked slowly round, intent on studying every detail. Leaning in over the offside door, I gazed in rapture at the instrument panel, and reached out to fondle the top of the gear lever.

Hearing the click of the shutter, I glanced up guiltily to see the Major standing close by, peering down into the viewfinder. He looked up for a moment. 'Get in. Sit in the driving seat.'

It was tempting.

'Go on,' he said, and glanced into the viewfinder again.

'No. It's O.K.' I took a pace backwards, feeling suddenly ashamed without having the least idea why.

The Major looked disappointed. 'Why not? You wanted to.'

I shook my head and started to walk back towards the garden. It was as if he had caught me doing something obscene.

'Jamie,' he called, striding quickly after me so as to catch up. 'There's something I'd like you to do for me.'

I glanced back apprehensively, scarcely daring to imagine what it might be. He stepped briefly into the house and reappeared a moment later carrying the bundle of clothes. He held them out towards me. 'I'd like you to put these on.'

I stared at him in amazement. 'Why?'

His face suddenly hardened. 'Because it would please me,' he said. 'Don't you think at least you owe me that?'

'Why can't I just get into my own clothes?'

'I've told you. I want you to wear these.'

They turned out to consist of a complete cricket outfit; flannels, socks, boots, white shirt, even a cap. They were clean, and neatly ironed, but obviously not new. All things considered, they were a tolerable fit.

The Major seemed to be in the grip of some intense emotion. 'Roll your sleeves up; just below the elbow.' He leant forward to adjust the angle of the cap, then took a pace back and stood gazing at me with his mouth open, his eyes screwed up a little as though he were trying to see through a mist. 'It's almost perfect,' he muttered.

I thought he was going to take some more photographs but the camera was nowhere to be seen. He simply stood and gazed at me, as if he were in a trance, occasionally shaking his head and whispering, 'Oh, Jamie.'

The church clock struck four. 'Can I go now?' I said. 'They'll be expecting me back.'

'What?' He came to with an effort. 'Oh. Yes. Yes, very well.' He motioned me vaguely towards the house. 'You'd better get changed.'

I was just doing up my shoelaces when he came into the study and picked up the cricket clothes from the floor, folding them neatly and placing them back on the chair seat. 'These were my son's,' he said. 'They've been lying in a drawer all this time. I suddenly thought I'd like to see a boy wearing them.'

'Why me?'

'Do you object? After all, both of us lost our loved ones in the war. Survivors have to help each other to make the best of things.'

It wasn't really an answer. Besides, there was something else bothering me about the sports kit, though I couldn't think what it was. I finished tying my laces and stood up, feeling more bewildered than ever but marginally more secure; at least I had my clothes on. Not that anything less than six inches of concrete would have made me feel safe with the Major.

'I hope I'll see you again very soon,' he said, as he opened the front door. Then, almost immediately, he closed it again and started to fumble in his pocket. 'Before you go, you'd better have this, if it means so much to you.' He fished out Andy's ten shilling note and slipped it into my hand.

I shot him one last look of speechless amazement, and fled.

'Well?' said Roy, as I walked into our Day Room. 'What did he do? More to the point, how much did you make?'

'What's it to you?'

He sniggered. 'Conduct unbecoming. Should be good for a new ping-pong set at the very least. Or did he just have you looking for pellets?'

'He's a nut case,' I said, and left it at that.

Later, when we were alone, I offered Andy the ten bob; but he wouldn't take it. So I paid for my window, got twenty Gold Flake with the change, and gave him half of them.

'You know what I reckon about the Major?' he said during the week, when we were chewing the rag over the events of Sunday. 'It wasn't a wife and son he lost; it was a couple of other things.' He drew his finger gently across my flies. 'If you ask me, he hasn't got what it takes.'

'That's a relief.'

Andy shook his head. 'Believe me, Jamie. Blokes like that can be the worst of all.'

It was hot, and we'd taken our shirts off. When it was time to go home I picked up Andy's by mistake. While we were swapping, I realised what had been puzzling me about the cricket clothes.

There should have been name tabs in them, and there weren't.

3.

For the next ten days, I lived in constant dread of being summoned again by the Major. As time passed, I began to hope that he might have thought the better of it; but the initial relief was gradually undermined by a strange uneasiness. There was no sense to it. My most fervent prayer had been that he should leave me completely alone; yet now he was doing so, there was a part of me that resented his neglect. When the call finally came, and it turned out that Roy was invited as well, I didn't know whether to think of him as an ally or a trespasser.

This time, we were supposed to go up for tea on Saturday afternoon and stay for the evening. When we arrived, the MG was parked at the front of the house instead of round the back.

Roy was patronising about my enthusiasm. 'Slick gear change; but the brakes aren't up to racing. They fade if you hammer them.'

'How do you know?'

'I've driven one. A couple, actually.'

'You're not old enough.'

'You can do what you like on private property.'

'Can you? I'd love to drive an MG.'

'I should have thought a pedal car was more your line.'

The Major led us through the house and out into the garden. For a moment, I thought he was going to make us play Bumblepuppy. The upright pole with its rope and captive ball had featured in one or two rather disturbing dreams since my last visit, and the sight of it made me vaguely uneasy.

'We'll have our tea out here. Nothing like a meal out of doors, what?'

The garden furniture had green stains advancing up its legs, and patches of rust where the white paint had chipped away. But in spite of this, the Major's tea time arrangements had the same air of forbidding elegance as his dining table. There were cakes on silver dishes amidst a vast profusion of doyleys; and the sandwiches, neat white rectangles with the crusts cut off, were like war graves, arranged in organised rows between symmetrical sprigs of parsley.

We sat on slatted chairs which wobbled disconcertingly on the uneven paving.

'I must say, this is extremely kind of you, sir,' said Roy.

The Major made a small gesture of deprecation. 'One does what one can to maintain civilised standards in the face of rationing and socialism.'

As I expected, Roy monopolised the conversation. He and the Major seemed made for each other, and it was plain that nothing I said would be of the least interest to either of them. Most of the time I kept my eyes well down, examining the crumbs on my plate, or watching insects explore the cracks between the flagstones. I began to wonder what I was there for. I suppose I'd mentally prepared myself for some sort of struggle; but against whom, against what? In any case, nothing seemed to be happening.

As the meal drew to a close, Roy leant forward and said discreetly, 'Excuse me, sir, I wonder if I could have a wash?'

'Yes, of course. You remember where it is?'

I realised too late that I should have gone after him.

'Excellent boy, that,' said the Major, as Roy disappeared into the house. 'Made of the right stuff. Good to know you've got such a splendid friend.'

A suitably diplomatic answer eluded me, so I sat in silence and squirmed.

The Major glanced shrewdly in my direction. 'I take it the pair of you do things together?'

I could scarcely believe my ears. Was he expecting to watch?

'No,' I said.

The Major seemed put out. 'Oh. Thought you'd probably go swimming, or make model aeroplanes, or whatever it is you do.'

'Oh, I see. Actually, I kick around with Andy mostly.'

He nodded, distantly. The idea seemed not to please him. 'Football and so on,' he muttered.

'Well, sometimes; yes.'

'But you spoke of kicking.' He seemed to think I was trying to mislead him.

I shrugged helplessly. 'It's just an expression. To kick around with someone.'

His eyes narrowed. 'Ah. That's what you call it.'

Luckily, before we could wallow any deeper into confusion, Roy appeared at the garden door again. The Major welcomed him back with an approving smile; you'd think he'd just been scoring a century instead of having a pee.

When it was clear that both of us had finished eating, the Major rubbed his hands together briskly and announced, 'Now. I know what Jamie wants.'

I looked up in alarm.

'Jamie wants to sit in the driving seat of the MG.'

Roy glanced round at me in scornful amusement.

'No, it's all right,' I mumbled, trying to cover my embarrassment. 'I don't really.'

'Yes, you do,' said the Major indulgently, 'and so you shall. Off you go now. You saw where it was parked. And while you're getting that out of your system, perhaps Roy would give me a hand with the tea things.'

'A pleasure, sir,' I heard Roy saying, as I set off towards the front of the house.

Dutifully, I walked all round the car, inspecting it from different angles, and then got into the driving seat. The door wouldn't open, so I had to clamber in over the side. I was disappointed to find that my heart didn't leap as I'd expected. A few days ago, when I hadn't dared to sit in it, the MG had throbbed with potential life, the perfect embodiment of beauty, power, and alluring mystery; but now I was actually gripping the steering wheel, the whole car seemed totally inert. I might as well have been sitting on a stuffed horse.

The keys weren't in the ignition, and in any case I wasn't entirely sure how you started the engine. Even then, I couldn't have driven it an inch. As usual, Roy had been right. I felt foolish and inadequate.

Of course, it wasn't the Major's fault. Whatever he wanted from me, at least he had tried to please me in return. Then I saw in a flash that I'd been missing the point. It had simply been an excuse to get me out of the way. No wonder nothing seemed to be happening; the main event was going on in the house. As Roy's friend, I might have been acceptable. As Andy's, I wasn't.

I climbed out of the car and sat on the grass a little distance away from it. I hated Roy. I hated the Major. I hated the car. If it had been standing on a cliff edge, I'd have let the handbrake off and pushed it over.

It must have been about half an hour before Roy appeared round the side of the house and summoned me indoors with a jerk of his head. He wasn't giving anything away, and I asked no questions, but our eyes met for a moment and he seemed to be offering some kind of truce. For the time being, at any rate.

'Problem,' said the Major. 'I have one guest ticket for the Air Display next weekend, and one spare seat in my car; but I have two young friends who I think might like to accompany me.' He smiled expectantly.

In perfect synchronism, each of us graciously deferred to the other.

'I also have a proposal for settling the matter,' he added, undoing the legs of a folding card table. 'Solo? Or Pontoon?'

We agreed on Pontoon. The Major placed a polished wooden box on the table and invited me to open it. Inside there were hundreds and hundreds of golden counters, like sovereigns and half-sovereigns, in troughs lined with blue velvet.

I gasped. 'Are they real?'

Roy glanced over my shoulder. 'Of course not, you twerp.'

All the same, they were the most beautiful things I had ever seen. I should have been quite happy just to sit and look at them, wafted into a world of immaculate green baize and subdued lighting, mysterious dark-eyed women glittering with diamonds, and powerful men in evening dress challenging Destiny at each turn of a card.

The Major smiled. 'A glass of wine, I think.' He left me to take the counters out of the box while he busied himself with a corkscrew. I thought he only meant the wine for himself, but a minute or two later he placed a full glass beside each of us. Even Roy was a little taken aback.

As card-room dramas go, our game of Pontoon with the Major would have cut little ice in Hollywood. A casual observer could scarcely have guessed what was actually going on. But the complexity of the situation both intrigued and appalled me.

It was a fair bet that a day out with the Major would include some dubious and unscheduled features, so it made sense to try and lose the game. On the other hand, when the horizons of daily life were bounded by school at one end of the road and the Urquharts' at the other, any chance of getting away was worth considering, whatever the deal. Besides, the chance to clamber about inspecting aircraft at close quarters was not something to be given up lightly. Any boy would have jumped at it, and there was the added incentive that it would put me one up on Roy. For once, I might even be able to silence him by speaking with absolute authority.

Not that I had sufficient skill as a card player to influence the outcome very much, one way or the other. In a fair contest, I should have lost the game through sheer incompetence. But Roy, as I judged from his uncharacteristic recklessness, was probably trying to lose it himself.

There was a further complication, which it took me a little while to grasp. At one point, when I'd lost heavily on the previous three or four hands, it looked as if the game would be over long before the agreed deadline of seven o'clock. But the Major suddenly staked an absurdly large sum and promptly lost it to me with a lack of subtlety that he made no attempt to disguise. Scooping up the pool of coins from the middle of the table, he held them out towards me in his cupped hands, paused two or three seconds for maximum effect, and then released them in a long voluptuous shower onto the table in front of me.

'More gold for Jamie,' he said, giving me a piercing smile.

From then on, he made a whole series of tactical interventions. I soon gave up any attempt to take the initiative, and resigned myself to letting Roy and the Major decide the outcome. By the end of the game I was playing quite mechanically, scarcely noticing what the cards were, and watching my pile of sovereigns grow or dwindle with a sense of complete detachment.

'Thirsty work,' said the Major at one point, refilling our glasses to the brim. I didn't like the wine very much, but it felt rather grand to be drinking it, and in front of Roy I didn't dare ask for anything else.

At seven o'clock, my stack of sovereigns was so much bigger than Roy's that I was declared the winner before we even counted them. Roy shrugged philosophically, acknowledging defeat with every appearance of good grace.

'Well done, Jamie, well done,' said the Major, as we sat back in our seats. 'A famous victory and a worthy winner. That's a big, beautiful pile of gold you've got there.'

Luckily, I was too light-headed to be embarrassed. Even so, I thought I detected a slight edge to his voice as he continued.

'You like gold, don't you Jamie, especially other people's. I hope you're satisfied?'

I nodded.

Peter Ryde

'Good. Because after all, nobody can expect two prizes. A pile of gold for Jamie; and a ticket to the Air Show for Roy.'

We glanced briefly at each other, and then stared at the Major, utterly nonplussed. He was sitting bolt upright, scanning our faces with obvious relish. 'There now,' he said. 'That's given you both something to think about.'

After a long pause, Roy swallowed hard and said 'I really don't think it's quite fair, sir.'

The Major turned towards him, granite faced. 'Do you not?'

'No, sir. After all, you said…'

'I said nothing. You assumed.'

We sat in silence for two or three minutes. I couldn't see the expression on Roy's face because I was staring at my feet. After a time, I glanced up and found the Major looking down at me intently.

'I dare say you think it's a hard lesson I've taught you, Jamie. I did offer you the quick and easy way, but you wouldn't take it. So you've had to learn it the slow and difficult way instead.'

There was another prolonged silence. Eventually Roy cleared his throat and said, glancing at his watch, 'I think we should be going now, sir.'

'I told Mrs Urquhart I should send you home at eight. I think some music would probably be appropriate. Jamie needs something to calm him after the storm.'

He produced a bulky album of gramophone records from a cupboard. Withdrawing them carefully from their sleeves, he placed the entire stack on the spindle of a massive autoplayer that stood in the corner. 'Now,' he said, 'you shall hear the two greatest singers who have ever lived.'

As the first record dropped with a thump onto the turntable, he motioned me to come-and sit beside him on the sofa. A moment or two later, he placed hi arm around my shoulder and drew me so close to him that I could see the individual threads of his shirt collar and smell the shaving soap on his smooth cheeks.

Except for the jerky interruptions of the autochanger every three or four minutes, the music seemed featureless and interminable. I could not even begin to imagine what it might be. A man and a woman were singing alternately in a foreign language, as if they were having a conversation; every time they stopped, a huge orchestra swelled up with overpowering intensity, sending the Major into spasms of quivering ecstasy, and causing the glass ornaments on the mantelpiece to rattle. His eyes were closed, and there was a look of infinite tenderness on his face, but his arm felt as rigid as a robot's and he gripped me with such crushing force that I could scarcely breathe.

After the last record finished, it was several minutes before the Major's hold began to slacken. As he slowly released me and I was able to draw away from him, I saw that tears had been trickling all down his face.

With astonishing alacrity, he snapped out of his trance. 'Right,' he said. 'Be off, the pair of you, or Mrs Urquhart'll be wondering what you've been up to.'

For once, Roy's command of etiquette seemed to have deserted him. He stepped out on to the front path without a word.

'Good night, Roy,' said the Major, pointedly, adding after a pause, 'Isn't there something you've forgotten?'

Roy felt all his pockets from the outside, and shook his head. 'No, I don't think so.'

'Oh? I do. So does James. Don't you, James?'

'The ticket?' I suggested.

'No, no, no!' the Major exclaimed impatiently. I'll keep that safe.'

I was still trapped inside the house, but by stepping to one side I was able to telegraph to Roy, shaking hands with myself behind the Major's back.

'Oh. Yes. Thank you very much for the… tea. And everything.' His voice sounded slurred.

The Major turned and looked down at me gravely. 'Goodbye, James,' he said, with an air of sad finality, as Christ might have said farewell to Judas.

As soon as we made it through the gate and onto the road, Roy and I broke into a run and didn't stop until we were a couple of hundred yards from home. Just round the corner from the Urquharts' there was a rickety wooden seat fixed to a big chestnut tree. By tacit consent, we sat there for a few minutes before going indoors.

'You all right?' said Roy.

I nodded, though as a matter of fact my head was feeling rather peculiar.

'Look, I'm sorry. I don't know what all that was about, but it was a lousy trick he played on you.'

'I'm well out of it. It's yourself you need to worry about.'

'Oh, I can handle him. But you're dead right about him being a nutter.'

There was something I needed to know. 'What happened after you cleared away the tea?'

'We talked. He said he had plans for me.'

There was more. I waited.

'Actually, if you must know, he wanted me to try on some clothes.'

'Cricket things?'
'How did you know?'
'And I suppose he told you they were his son's?'
There was a long silence.
'We'd better go in,' I said.

4.

A week later, first thing in the morning, the Major collected Roy, and they set off together for the Air Display. With it being a Sunday, the rest of us were still in the process of getting up, but Andy and I stood at the window, half-dressed, and watched them go.

It was the last we ever saw of them.

By ten o'clock that night, they still hadn't returned or sent any message, so Mrs Urquhart rang up the Police. Next morning, miles out into the countryside, a couple of farm workers found the wreckage of an MG with the bodies of a man and a boy close by. The front end of the car had knocked a hole through the side of a brick barn.

There seemed to be no logical explanation for the accident. A policeman giving evidence at the inquest said that the car appeared to have been driven at high speed straight into the wall.

THE ARVON FOUNDATION
Residential Writing Courses

Spend time away from the pressures of home and work, and sample the unique Arvon experience. Four-and-a-half-day courses for beginners and more experienced writers in fiction, poetry and writing for radio, TV and stage. Expert, intensive tuition in our beautiful centre half way down a Pennine valley, near Hebden Bridge. Tutors this year include Stan Barstow, Hilary Mantel and Will Self. We also have centres in Devon and Scotland.

Please contact us for our comprehensive 1993 brochure.

ARVON AT LUMB BANK
HEPTONSTALL
HEBDEN BRIDGE
WEST YORKSHIRE HX7 6DF
☎ (0422) 843714

Supported by North West Arts Board

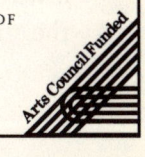

NOT MAKING IT

Annie Wright

You mother them, or try to, stroppy adolescents
coming in all hours, moody, uncommunicative,
's'alright the highest accolade, their own space
a stinking pit. You shout. You shout a lot.
You wish you didn't. They do something
crass, brick through a window, liberating
a boat, the stupid sods are not sorry.
You are furious, shout more. They skip school;
you didn't expect qualifications, but at least
you thought you knew where they were all day.
The rebel in you helps them rip their jeans,
punk their hair. You still kiss them goodnight.
You get depressed. They notice, make a brew,
ask if you're *alright*? You can't stay cross.
The summons comes for piracy; you're laughing.
Making up you cry, wish it could be better.
When they, and you, have gone too far
you miss the late night talks
in the fire's half-light, when they let
a few bruised dreams emerge, asked
what it's really like to be a woman,
to be in love, to do it. Sprawled out
you saw it in their eyes, brown, blue,
always beautiful, a look that had seen
the crack where two worlds meet.

Annie Wright

So much wasted time, so much shit to edit out
before the bad bend on a wet road, the little
leap, the head-on smack, the overdose,
the end in intensive care – you try
not to see it as reproach.

CANADIAN BOUYWAA

Matthew Caley

The child that crawls
        through a clump of crocuses
as big as a jar of celery
        thinks it is the African veldt.
With his skinny grazed knees
        he has the look of a soiled choirboy.
Three sisters occupy
        his peripheral blur. Two are Red Indians,
for Red Indians live in Africa, one is a foetus
        kicking inside a Laura Ashley balloon.
There are real cowboys, even now,
        he knows, they carry girders,
mend fences, advertise cigarettes.
        The sycamore he can only
yet dream of climbing lets its shadow
        fall across his hiding place.
His blue-striped T-shirt becomes camouflage.
        He is in someone else's
peripheral blur. She will be there
        when the tyger springs.

Canadian Bouywaa crouches
        next to him. That helps. Though the
child suspects he might not be
        that reliable when it comes to a fight.
Canadian Bouywaa is hard to define
        which is one of his charms.

One sister had stepped on him
        as she descended the stairs and the child
had cried for days. Somehow, unnoticed even by himself,
        there had been a resurrection
of sorts. For now Canadian Bouywaa crouches next to him
        on the African veldt and waits
for Red Indians or the tyger. whichever
        comes first. Tygers, the child suspects,
tygers usually get the jump on
        everyone. Even cowboys. The crocus
patch feels suddenly small. The child
        swivels to take in his father
who is a little way off, tugging at a tree-
        root and losing. He gauges the distance

between them, stopping at the intersection
        of Coldharbour Lane and Electric Avenue,
its dealer-strewn curbs. He wants to cross
        to the shops for cigarettes. The sycamore
he can only yet dream of climbing
        lets its shadow fall across his face.
That night he will share a bath
        with someone else's girlfriend
who tells him he has the body of a
        soiled choirboy. He is still in
someone else's peripheral blur. Will
        she be there when the tyger springs
She is hard to define which
        is one of her charms. Women always
get the jump on everyone. Especially poets. He buys
        crocuses for the squat.
Soon he will type out a poem

about Red Indians and a Laura Ashley
balloon. It will not include Canadian Bouywaa
who is still crouched on the African veldt, waiting.

SCORPION
Wang Jiaxin

I had turned over every stone on the hillside
without seeing a single scorpion: That was
which day? which year of my childhood?
And today I return to this hillside,
where the pines of my youth now are thick and tall, and out
from the midst of its reddish-brown, from a crack in a rock,
a single scorpion, stinger held high,
comes walking towards me.

We stare at one another, and in that moment
I become the sand and stone beneath its feet.

CHANGE

Wang Jiaxin
translated by John Cayley

The season changes
overnight.
Before you have time to prepare
the wind has slapped you in the face,
the wind has turned so cold you daren't go out.
You turn around. Miraculously
the sky has cleared to blue
under the buffets of the wind.

You are suddenly old,
worn out, your face unrecognisable.
You walk with difficulty through
    swirling piles of fallen leaves.
Just one night of fierce howling
and the wooden pail of your body is emptied.
As you walk
it rocks and sounds hollowly.

And the wind still bellies through the season.
The wind blows away the clouds.
The wind makes the sky higher, farther from you.
The wind is always seeing something off.
The wind is, under the tiles, in every muted place,
blowing. It is that urgent.

The days remaining are already running out.
Leaves fly off.
The sound of the wind in the trees,
the feeble sound of people and vehicles in the distance,
all pointed in one direction.

So pressing,
the wind has blown right into the spaces between your bones.
Just one night
and all is changed.
You were inwardly startled.
Pull yourself up. Now is the time
to hold out and face the wind, or else
        give up completely.

EMPTY VALLEY

Wang Jiaxin
translated by John Cayley

No one. In this lonely expanse
        there is nothing but wind
            and a crop of stones which covers the earth.

But when you come into the valley, you feel
        it has been waiting for you,
            that it is drawing round you like a slowly closing
                          palm.

Panic-stricken you run back, only daring to look back
        once you've reached the valley mouth. It is empty,
                absolutely empty
apart from wind, apart from stones.

STAIRWAY

Wang Jiaxin
translated by John Cayley

Each time, I
climb this hazardous stairway, with slow steps
circling upward, reaching the top,
switching on the light.

It is a ritual I return to,
led upwards in the darkness by the stairway
step by step, just as before.
And what if I did not take out my keys at the doorway
but raised my hand

to knock
as if there were someone waiting for me
inside the room – perhaps
my former self
would open the darkness.

HOMELAND

Wang Jiaxin
translated by John Cayley

When I am drawn down into the flowing waters, you are
a stone, deeply tanned and lying in the sun.

When I open the map
you have risen up into the sky.

When I have reached the border, and all but crossed over
your call comes to me from far away.

When I turn my head
the teeth of this century grip my throat.

WHY ENGLAND?

Judi Benson

I came here for the damp drizzlie days and postage stamp
gardens side by side in a long row of washing.
For weak tea and tanic acid staining the teeth.

I came for the paper-thin sandwiches, bangers and mash
Eel pie and phone charges for calls across the street.
I came for the cricket and the carnage of tame rabbits.

I came for the bowlers and the brollies poking the eye
for the pigeons, the tits on page three, the bum and fart jokes
the tipsy queen-mum, the dilapidated health care.

I came for the velvet flock, for Boxing Day and lace curtains.
For cardboard houses, the beggars, the buskers
the water closets, the closing hours, the trains not running.

I came for the bank charges, the leaseholds, the pit bulls
the minis and volvos, the driving tests, the wheel clamps
the pollution, the community care, the dinghy clinics.

I came for the pale nervous men with greasy hair
sad watery eyes begging to be beaten with raspberry tarts.
I came for the black pudding and the concrete tower blocks,

the take-aways on the high street, the bluejeans
off the back of a lorry, and the constant never-ending
use of the word sorry, to the door, to the lamppost.

WHYA NOT EAST HAM?

Judi Benson

An archaeologist friend recently said our house reminded him of a ship and these are all the things that have washed up on the beach. This could also apply to its inhabitants, if you want to stretch the truth. Jacksonville, Florida is a long way away but then the Atlantic is a mighty ocean and my father was a Navy Captain, so it explains my being in East Ham as well as anything else.

I've had a hard enough time explaining why I came to this country in the first place, not to mention why I've stayed here for fourteen years, so don't interrogate me about East Ham. I am likely to adopt a Neopolitan shrug and say whya not?' – everybody's gotta live somewhere, don't they?

Truth is, it's the only part of London we could afford, having tried Crouch End and Hornsey in the North and Tooting Bec in the south. The West didn't even get a look-in as we knew it was well out of our price range. Actually East Ham is a bit like me, neither one thing nor the other. Until 1971 it wasn't even London, but Essex. And well before that it was agricultural, considered quite posh by some who had their country estates out here where the air was fresh, away from the noisy, filthy, overcrowded city. Or so some like Katherine Frye believed. But the city just keeps moving eastwards.

You can't hear the Bow bells from here, so it's not strictly the East End, nor are we Docklands. You do hear Cockney, but nowadays you're just as likely to hear Bengali, Urdu, Kurdish, West Indian, Turkish and, if I speak, American. So we're quite cosmopolitan.

So what has East Ham got to offer? Six months ago we had two libraries, the sort that stock their shelves with crime fiction and how-to books in BIG PRINT. Thanks to a Nalgo strike we currently have no libraries. We did have swimming baths but these have been closed down for the usual reasons. Bookshops? If you consider W.H. Smith's a bookshop you could say we have one. We've no end of cheap shops, mostly clothing stores, charity shops and infant wear. By cheap, I don't just mean low prices.

We have several eel pie and mash shops though there's no longer any eel involved, just the 'liquor'. If you do want to splash out on a meal, your choices are Tandoori, Pizza Hut, McDonalds, more Tandoori, Chinese take-away, kebabs or a quasi-Italian restaurant which features 'authentic Egyptian belly dancers'. Of course there are a few fish and chip shops, the best being run by a jolly Chinese lady and on the week-ends there are vendors with cockles and winkles and other slimey things. We have several big markets and fruit and veg stalls, served up with a sharp wit and traditional East End humour, not to mention street vendors who mysteriously appear and disappear with their back-of-a-lorry goods – three lighters for a pound, leather jackets, handkerchiefs – whatever has washed ashore.

There are two nice parks, but for some inexplicable reason they've just torn down the tennis courts in one of them. But then they're busy tearing everything down these days. Twenty perfectly good terraced houses which have been standing for well over a hundred years have just been levelled – for what? A parking lot, of course. After all, that's what we really need. We do have several bingo halls for the desperate bleary-eyed purple rinse set. But there is no cinema, theatre, or gallery.

We've got loads of pubs, lovely to look at, but we seldom frequent any of them as they've turned into amusement arcades with blinking boisterous machines and over-loud music served up with over-priced pints – but that's London innit?

Schools here are a shambles and if your dad's not a plumber or mechanic you've got no chance. So most lads leave school for the dole and the dubious occupation of hanging about on street corners, while the girls opt out for early motherhood. Course there's always crime as a way of earning a bob or two.

We are famous for our football ground, West Ham, which is only a stone's throw from here. Not being a football supporter it isn't a selling point for me. Days when there's a game on, the cheering sounds very much like the sea coming in over the pebbles – or so I tell myself. Personally we've never had any bother, partly because we live in a cul de sac buffeted from the busy Barking Road by council flats. I've no doubt there's plenty of thieving goes on round here but we don't tend to steal from our own and in fact the only time

I've ever had my bag pinched was in a swanky hotel in Russell Square. While West End taxi drivers are loathe to come out here late at night, it is equally true that East End cabbies don't cotton to going 'down London'.

It's taken nearly ten years for our neighbours to get friendly, and we no longer squabble over a half inch of boundary or our cats getting into their garden. In fact, they welcome our free-range rabbit who helps herself to their vegetation and is even rewarded with biscuits. And most people have stopped asking me how long I'm over here for, so I feel accepted in an off-beat beat-up anonymous kind of way, which I prefer to being cloned with other Americans in Hampstead or Knightsbridge or Sloane Square.

We do have public transport, or I should say, as I write this we do, though our bus garage is on the list to be axed. And if you don't care about surviving, we do have a hospital...

What we do have is a sense of community, albeit in a small radius, and we do look after our own. Though sadly more and more of the older generation are dying off and with them the history of the place. Nobody has got very much, which is also why I feel more comfortable here than I would in my own country where it is nigh on to a crime not to have at least two cars and three microwaves, which you have to work all hours to obtain. No one round here talks about what they do, it's basic, you either have work or you don't. We keep ourselves to ourselves.

As a Navy brat, I've lived in more places than I have fingers and toes, and seldom stayed anywhere longer than two years. I don't claim any of those places and none of them claimed me, though each left an impression. I always envied people who, when asked where they were from, could give an answer, and who felt it truly was the explanation of who they were, why they were the way they were. My answer sounds like a jigsaw puzzle and explains nothing. So I get sarcastic now and say I come from my mama who is a southern aristocrat from Macon, Georgia, another place I do not claim.

The happiest time of my life was spent living in London from 1954 to 1956, a good time to be on American military salary, while the rest of the country was still on rations. The family was all together then, for the last time in fact, and I was blissfully a little girl exploring a strange and exciting city. It was the last time I felt I belonged anywhere so in a sense I came back here in 1978 to find that little girl with her sense of well-being.

Let's face it, truth is, I live in my ship of a house or in my head, with a wild garden out back full of herbs and flowers regularly pruned by our rabbit. The Russian vine is on its way to covering the house and the sharp saw grass (pinched from Bridlington beach) helps keep intruders out. It's astoundingly quiet most of the time, and most of the time the phone doesn't even ring.

Ideally I'd live in the middle of nowhere in the Yorkshire Dales with cows and sheep as neighbours. Failing that, I paint pictures of such places, close my curtains and pretend. From the outside we are any terraced house with net curtains. From the inside, well, it's a ship innit? Who knows, maybe it will float, along with the floating pound, when this country finally does go down the drain.

Panurge

Where did Patrick McCabe (Booker shortlist), Kathy Page (Methuen) and many others make their U.K. debuts? **PANURGE**. How do we find the nerve to print 12,000 word stories by completely unknown writers? **NEW WRITING**. Why does Peter Lewis think small publishers will save us from oblivion in the '90s? **NEW FEATURES**. What makes literary agents and London publishers keep on subscribing? **NEW WRITERS**. What is the intriguing theme of the Short Story Competition with cash prizes and some mystery prizes? (Send s.a.e. for details). **NEW COMPETITIONS** plus many more surprises.

Why not subscribe at the Bargain Introductory Rate? 35% off! Only £6.50 for *two* handsome paperbacks (current and next issues). Abroad: £7 surface, £9 airmail.

NEW EDITOR John Murray won the Dylan Thomas Award for short stories in 1998. He founded Panurge in 1984.

PANURGE, Crooked Holme Farm Cottage,
Brampton, Cumbria, U.K.
☎ 06977–41087

THE CITY OF ETERNAL YOUTH

Stephen Gregory

Potosi, Bolivia

When I got off the train at Potosi, I was met on the platform by a policeman. At least he said he was a policeman; I didn't believe him. He was short and elderly, in baggy jeans and a dirty anorak. His thick stubble was grey; tufts of greasy grey hair stuck out of the greasy green baseball cap he was wearing.

'Police,' he said, blocking my way along the platform. He waved some sort of official-looking identification card at me, with a little photograph on it, but then he put it back in his pocket before I could look at it. 'Police,' he said. 'I need to see your passport. I need to see all the money and travellers cheques you're carrying.'

I was very tired and cold. The train journey from La Paz to Potosi had taken thirteen hours. A fine journey, yes. There was scrub-desert as far as Oruro, a grim, windswept, tin-mining town, where the train stopped for diesel in an oily station yard. Then the shimmering salt-flats of Lake Poopo; flamingos, brilliantly pink on the glare of white, and flocks of geese and coot. More desert, of tussocky grass scoured by sand; falcons, hunched and moustachioed like gangsters, perched on the telegraph poles along the line. The train climbed into khaki crags, until the barren brown landscape was creased with ice and snow. The carriage filled with dust. By nightfall, the air grew thinner and breathlessly cold. A fine journey, but I was glad to arrive in Potosi. I wanted hot food and hot coffee and a warm bed in a clean hotel – not a good time for a ragged little thief to pretend he was a policeman so that he might get his hands on my money.

'Show me your identification, please, señor,' I said, as patiently as I could. 'I didn't see it just then. Show me again, please.'

He blocked my way, stepping to left and right to try and stop me from walking along the platform. All the other passengers had hurried off, bundled in blankets and ponchos. The train had been shunted into a siding. Someone was turning off the station lights. It was ten o'clock on a bitter, black, Bolivian night. My ears and lips and nostrils were freezing. My eyelashes were caked with dust. Twelve thousand feet above sea-level, my patience was as thin as the air.

'Police,' the man said again. 'You've seen my identification. Show me your money. I'll need to take it to the police-station for tests. Sometimes we find traces of cocaine on American dollar bills. I'll give you a receipt of course.'

He held out a cracked hand, ingrained with dirt.

My journey through the Andean countries of South America would soon be over. My money was almost gone. After nine months' travelling, with a little experience of Peruvian and Bolivian bandits, I thought this was the silliest ploy I'd heard so far.

'I don't believe what you've told me, señor,' I said. 'You say you're a policeman? I think you are not. You want to take all my dollars, to test my fingerprints for cocaine? I think you're a thief. Excuse me, please. I'm very cold and very tired.'

Saying this, I jabbed him once on the chest with the tip of my left forefinger. He staggered a few paces backwards and, crying out loudly, sat down on the platform. But there was no-one to hear him. This – his second ploy – went completely unnoticed.

Having failed to get my money one way, now he lay on the ground and moaned as though I'd hit him, hoping either for my sympathy or that someone would come and remonstrate on his behalf. He lay there and coughed terribly. Stepping over him, I strode along the deserted platform, showed my ticket to a man who was huddled over a paraffin heater in a lamplit cubicle, and climbed away from the station towards the lights of the town itself.

Early in the 17th century, Potosi was the richest city in the world. With a population of 150,000, it was bigger than London or Paris. The Spaniards found vast amounts of silver in the Indian workings in Cerro Rico, the hill on which the city was built. Using Indian slave labour to extract it, they built a mint and many fine churches and mansions. However, when the silver began to run out and other mines were opened in Peru and Mexico, Potosi lost its importance to the Spaniards and became something of a ghost-town.

I woke the following morning in the Hotel IV Centenario, a huge, echoing building opened on the fourth centenary of the Spaniards' founding of Potosi on April 10th, 1545. My room was bare and cold, but there were lashings of scalding water in the bathroom. The sun poured through the tall windows; the air swirled with silvery specks of dust as I sprang out of bed. Somewhere, hundreds of yards away, the pipes clanged and whistled when I turned on the taps. As I dressed, scrubbed pink and carefully shaved, I looked into the street markets in the square outside the hotel, across the sandy brown roofs of the town, to the crinkled, sandy brown mountain which had brought so much wealth and so much misery to Potosi. Behind it, the sky was as blue as a starling's egg.

Although the sun was warm where I sat among the yew hedges in the plaza de armas, the fountain had frozen solid; in the shade of narrow, winding, cobbled streets, there were sheets of ice nearly six inches thick. A brass band was playing. I wandered about the town, marvelling at the crumbling mansions still emblazoned with the crests and mottoes of the grandees who'd lived there. Shadows whispered, cobwebs fluttered and the floorboards groaned, as I tiptoed into churches which the Spaniard had built. The gloom was relieved by the gleam of silver, bright in the candlelight. I visited the mint: high, dark rooms panelled with Spanish oak, in which vast wooden wheels and cogs and presses were once worked by donkeys and Indians. I drank big bowls of coffee and ate chicken saltenas in a shabby, warm restaurant, and then I went walking again.

Piglets and black, hairless dogs rooted in rubbish-tips by the railway line. Indians shivered in corrugated-iron shanties. Locomotives made in Langley Mill rusted in the sidings, like long-dead dinosaurs. Old American saloon cars rumbled through cheerless markets. Then I returned to the same restaurant for more coffee and more salteñas.

Walking to keep warm, in bare, barren, bitter Potosi! Dead stone houses silvered with frost! Dead cobbled streets sheeted with ice! Dry, thin air; dry, thin people with sun-reddened faces, frost-bitten fingers, thin lips and pinched nostrils! Cold! Wherever I walked, wherever I huddled and dozed, the mountain was always there. It looked like nothing: nothing but a crinkled, sandy brown hill. It was the lode that had lured the Spaniard to Potosi, that made it the richest city in the world.

That evening, malt beer and pollo picante with Jamie Holloway, a radio presenter from Austin, Texas. He was waiting to catch the overnight bus to

La Paz.

'It'll be bloody cold,' I warned him. 'Take your sleeping-bag out of your rucksack before they load the bus – you'll need it. Once your rucksack is tied on to the roof with all the other passengers' luggage, you won't have another chance to get it down. You've got a sleeping-bag, I suppose?'

I was enjoying my role as the smug, seasoned traveller; young Jamie had only been in South America a week. He'd flown into La Paz, stayed for the fiesta, and come south to Potosi.

'And now I gotta head straight back to La Paz!' he said. 'What a waste of fucking time! If I see that bastard before I get out of this town, I'll fucking kill him!'

Jamie was upset. He told me he'd been greeted on the railway platform at Potosi by an elderly little man in ragged jeans and a dirty anorak, whose greasy grey hair stuck out of a greasy green baseball cap.

'He said he was a policeman! He showed me his identification!'

'Did you read it?' I asked.

'No, I didn't read it!' the Texan said. 'I showed him my passport and he gave it back to me. I gave him my money and he wrote me a receipt.'

'And this morning?'

'This morning I went to the police station, showed them the receipt and asked for my money.'

'And they laughed?'

'Yes, they fucking laughed!'

I tried not to laugh, but I couldn't help smiling. 'How much did you give him, the so-called policeman? I know you've told me once already... tell me again please, Jamie! I can't believe it! Tell me again and, in return, I'll pay for the beer!'

'I gave him $300, you smug English bastard! Three hundred US dollars, cash!'

So I paid for the beer and chicken – the least I could do – and I walked Jamie Holloway to the bus station. He had just enough for his fare to La Paz, where he'd either wire home for more money or abandon his South American journey and fly back to the States, using his return ticket. Fuming, furious, as fierce-looking as the moustachioed falcons I'd seen on the altiplano, he stared at every little, old, stubbly-faced man we passed, and glared at every baseball cap.

I waved him off. Having resisted the temptation to describe my own meeting with the bogus policeman on Potosi railway station, how I'd knocked him to the ground with a single blow.

The following night I went inside the silver mountain.

Wilbert, my guide, was a muscular fellow with flopping black hair and a wide smile. I would have said he was thirty-five years old, about my age. He told me he was thirteen. Our taxi climbed among smoke-filled, firelit shanties on the outskirts of Potosi – where piglets snuffled in oily slime, where wretched drunks slithered on sheets of ice, where dogs chased alongside us, snarling at the windows – and dropped us on the bare hillside, high above the town. It was a howling, black night. I was wearing all the clothes I had, with a scarf wrapped round my head. As I watched the taxi's warm red tail-lights disappearing, Wilbert seized my hand and tugged me towards a huddle of huts.

'This is the mine manager's hut, señor Stephen!' he shouted to me, above the wind. 'We're going to see one of the private mines inside the mountain – all of the mines are private, run by co-operatives, except for the two big state-owned mines. It's more interesting for you to see a little mine, worked in exactly the same way it was worked by slaves in the days of the Spaniards. Nothing much has changed since then. Come this way, señor, and I'll introduce you to the manager!'

Inside the tiny hut, where the manager had been asleep on a bed, I had to sign a visitor's book and pay a fee of seven bolivianos. The manager smeared his eyes, fitted another plug of coca into his gums, and equipped me with a helmet and a little gas lamp. He lay down again, as soon as Wilbert took my hand and led me from the hut into the mouth of the mine.

It was cold at first, although we were out of the wind straightaway. I whacked my head on the low tunnel; the impact jammed the helmet onto my glasses and knocked them off my face. We walked and walked and soon the air grew warmer. I adjusted the flame of my lamp, which fluttered and faded. There was wet mud underfoot, between wooden rails. The further we went – as I followed Wilbert for five, ten, fifteen minutes into the mountain – the lower we bent. Soon the tunnel was tiny and I dropped to my hands and knees. This made it hard to move forward and hold the lamp at the same time. Hotter and hotter, hard to breathe – gasping at Wilbert to stop for a moment, I knelt in the mud and tore the scarf from my throat, wrestled out of my jacket and one of the three pullovers I was wearing and tied them all clumsily around my waist. So we continued, writhing on our bellies through a tunnel no more than three feet high.

White mud, glistening hole. Wilbert's boots in front of my face, dragging myself forward, trying to hold up my lamp, slithering in milky sludge-water, hotter and hotter and hotter until I could hardly breathe. Can't turn round, can't go back, helmet banging on rocks, lamp gone out, sweat and mud in my eyes! Can't see can't breathe can't move can't get out please help me get out please I can't...

Wilbert had somehow managed to turn towards me and was dragging me by the wrists into a chamber where I sat up and heaved and heaved until I could breathe again.

Wilbert waited for me to recover, and then he said, 'This is Tio. He owns the mine.'

Carved in the rock, there was an effigy of the devil, with horns and teeth and a long pointed tail. He was lit by a dozen candles. The chamber was splattered with wax. The miners had left gifts for him – cigarettes, coca leaves, coins, coffee and tea.

'Tio owns the mountain and all the silver in it,' Wilbert said. 'He always has done. The Spaniard sent us inside the mountain and made us work as his slaves, but he never owned it. Tio owns it. Once we are inside the mine, we work for him – not for the Spaniard. Leave a gift for him, señor, so that we will get out safely, and then we'll go a little further. If you listen carefully now, you'll hear that someone is working, somewhere in the mine, although it's late on a Saturday night. We'll go and see who it is.'

I opened my money-belt, took out some of the letters I'd collected in the British embassy in La Paz, tore off the stamps and placed them among the dried-up coca leaves. Wilbert nodded his approval. We held our breath and listened, and we heard a faint tapping deeper in the mountain, the muffled ringing of iron on rock.

'Yes, someone is still working tonight,' the boy whispered. He smiled to see me so wet and hot and so filthy. 'Let's go and find him, señor Stephen. The miners have lived and worked in these tunnels for four hundred years. I'm sure you can manage just one visit...'

We slithered on our bellies for another ten minutes. I'd had time as we rested with Tio, the avuncular devil, to arrange and re-tie the clothes around my waist, to re-light my lamp and wipe my glasses – so the going was tolerable. The hammering grew louder until at last we broke into another chamber, no bigger than Tio's chamber, where a man was working. The three of us squatted together.

The miner was Pedro Cabrera. His shoulders, chest and arms were powerfully muscled: stripped to the waist, he wore cheap, thin trousers and flimsy, plastic shoes. He didn't speak a word to us, although he seemed glad to rest while we were there. He'd been driving a hole into the rock face so that a dynamite charge could be inserted the following week. Now he grinned at me, without speaking. The heat was overwhelming. Pressed to the walls and ceiling of the tiny, lamplit cavern, we poured with sweat. Pedro had been in the hole all day, from ten in the morning until now, seven in the evening – entirely alone, without eating or drinking, alone with his hammers and a pocketful of coca.

'The coca is not addictive,' Wilbert told me, while Pedro Cabrera gazed at me with eyes as wet and brown as a cow's. 'But it's customary. Everybody uses it. It relieves hunger and thirst and tiredness. It limits boredom. It helps the concentration. Pedro can work in here as much or as little as he likes, clocking in and out at the manager's hut – as part of the co-operative, he's paid for the good ore he brings out. It's better than the days of 'la mita'.'

Wilbert waited for me to ask him what 'la mita' was. I asked him and he went on.

'It was a period of twenty years worked in the mines, in the days when the Spaniard used Indian slaves to bring out the silver. The Indians lived and worked in the mines. By law, they worked in the mountain for four month periods, without coming out at all, for up to twenty years. For four months at a time they lived in the mountain and never saw the sun or the stars, never breathed the fresh air. A slave who fulfilled 'la mita' – his twenty-year service – was called a 'mitayo'. We still use the name for someone who's worked all his life in the mountain.'

He paused to let me try and understand all this. Then he continued, while all the time the miner gazed at me and chewed, like a great gormless cow.

'Things are better now, of course, although the work itself is just as it was in the terrible days of the Spaniard. The miners work long and hard to feed themselves and their families. The silver is harder and harder to find. They start work when they are twelve or thirteen and continue until they are thirty-five or forty. I myself have been lucky so far, señor – instead of working in the mines, as my father did, I work as a guide, bringing visitors to see inside. All the miners have silicosis – all of them, without exception. As soon as they can get a doctor's certificate to say they have 60% silicosis, they can retire at once, with a pension. They get a better pension if they have 80% silicosis. Generally, the miners die in their forties, if they've worked in the mountain for twenty years or so. You don't see any old men in Potosi, señor Stephen –

for this reason, they call it "el pueblo de la juventud eterna" – the city of eternal youth!'

Pedro Cabrera, who hadn't looked as though he was listening to anything Wilbert was saying, chuckled at this. It was a good joke; he'd heard it many times before. For a few seconds his eyes were alive. Then they clouded, deadened by years of dust and years of coca. He grinned at me, showing yellow teeth and brown gums, and he shook my hand. Before I'd knelt down and followed Wilbert into the tunnel, the man was working again, banging with hammer and spike, deepening the hole he was drilling for next week's dynamite.

We writhed and wriggled on our bellies, clutching our gas lamps, knocking our helmets on the rock. We stopped for a minute with Tio, to pay our respects again. 'He owns the mountain, señor Stephen, and, while we are inside it, he owns us too,' Wilbert said. The candles were burning low; the flames danced, as the cavern fluttered with little gasps of air. A cooler draught whispered in the tunnel, rustling the coca leaves at the devil's feet. The stamps I'd left were already splashed with wax. Wilbert said goodbye to Tio, thanking him for a safe passage. As we crept closer and closer to the surface, we felt an icy wind on our faces. Soon we could stand up. Soon the air was freezing. We stepped into a howling black night, on a hillside riddled with mines – for four hundred years, men had burrowed and bellied inside it, like wasps in an apple.

Without waking the manager, we left our helmets and lamps in his hut. Bundled in all my clothes again, I followed Wilbert down the hill – there was no hope of a taxi, up there. The lights of Potosi twinkled below us. The stars were bright above us. The air nipped at my nose, and my breath was silver in front of my face, but I warmed up as I tried to keep pace with Wilbert. After an hour of slithering down the steep, dark slope, we came to the shanties. Wilbert kept the dogs from us, cracking them expertly on the top of the head with a knobby stick he'd picked up. The track was treacherously icy. The corrugated-iron huts were wretched; wrapped in cardboard and newspaper, people were sleeping on banks of dirty snow. Wilbert marched ahead of me, as though he didn't want me to see these things – he'd said that things were better for the miners since the days of 'la mita'. And so we came to the outskirts of Potosi itself: the narrow, cobbled streets and sturdy houses; the bright, well-stocked corner shops where people sat and stared as we walked by. Good smells of frying meat and fresh bread and strong, hot coffee.

Wilbert asked me into his family house – we stood at the door as I paid him the $5 he asked for – but I declined his invitation, although the kitchen looked warm and snug and I was tempted to go inside. I was anxious to return to my hotel room so that I could get out of my filthy wet clothes and into that scalding shower. Wilbert nodded: he could see I was starting to shiver, now that we'd stopped walking fast downhill. Hearing us talking at the door, Wilbert's little brothers and sisters came to look at me, peering past his legs to see the gringo he'd taken to the mine. At Wilbert's request, I opened my money-belt, took out some more postage stamps and gave them to the children. They thanked me politely and disappeared; clearly, they were used to seeing the foreigners their big brother took inside the mountain.

About to leave, I shook the guide by the hand. But, just then, an old man's face loomed over Wilbert's shoulder. He must have heard our voices too, and come to see who was standing on the cold doorstep. The man stared at me for a long second, as though he couldn't quite recognise me. I recognised him straightaway; he was small and stubbly, wearing a greasy green baseball cap on greasy grey hair. He stared for a long long second, until his eyes flickered with alarm and he quickly withdrew to the warmth of the kitchen. I heard him barking at Wilbert, to close the door and lock it, and then I heard him coughing. The boy frowned, suddenly dropping my hand.

'Who's the old man?' I asked the boy, as he began to close the door on me. 'I've seen him in the town. Indeed, he was the first person to greet me when I got off the train at Potosi station.'

The boy flushed very deeply. He didn't answer. Somewhere in the house, the man was still coughing – coughing and spitting and coughing again.

'The old man… is he your father?' I asked. 'Does he greet all the gringos like that, when they arrive on the train from La Paz?'

Still the boy said nothing. The coughing continued.

'Is he ill?' I persisted. 'The old man, who makes such a warm welcome for the foreigners who come to Potosi?'

At last the boy flared at me, but he controlled his voice and spoke very softly. His anger and his shame were worse like that.

'Yes, señor, he waits for the gringos who get off the train! And some of them are stupid enough to believe what he tells them! Like me, he lives off the gringos now. It's better and easier than digging in the mountain! And yes, señor, of course my father is ill! Didn't you listen, señor, when I explained to you? He's a "mitayo"! He's not an old man! He's forty! Didn't you listen, señor? There are no old men in Potosi!'

He slammed the door.

It was very cold in the street. There was frost on the cobbles. I walked quickly to the Hotel IV Centenario. When I collected my key at reception, the manager stared at my clothes which were whitened with mud from the mine. My hair was white with dust, plastered to my head. The hotel corridors were no warmer than the streets – an icy draught blew in the long, dark tunnels, picking up dust from threadbare carpets. But when the pipes clanked, when I turned on the tap in the bathroom, the water was almost too hot to hear.

Later, scrubbed pink and raw, I pummelled myself dry with a towel and got ready to climb into my sleeping-bag, inside the bed. The mountain was silver in the moonlight. The streets were quiet and still, gleaming with frost. A few lorries stood silent, sheeted with tarpaulin. Looking down into the square, I saw people under the market-stalls, settling for the night, swaddled in blankets and ponchos, huddled together for warmth. Somebody was coughing. That was the only sound in the dead, cold town. I went to bed, but the coughing kept me awake for a long time.

RADIO ACTIVITY

John Murray

How would you like to roam the wide globe courtesy of a very special, indeed magical, radio valve? Shuttling between, for example, Sellafield and Morocco while enjoying interference from Radio Tangiers, Radio Cumbria and an hilarious Sudeten-German-Cumbrian P.O.W., Klaus Asbach? And an even madder Tangerine poet called Moulay Ismail?

It's 1986, the year of Chernobyl. It's the Biggest Liar in the World Competition, just downwind from Sellafield. It's John Murray's *Radio Activity*.

'a fine writer' – *Daily Telegraph*
'a real gift for comic and abusive exaggeration' – *London Magazine*

Retail price £7.99. Subscribers to Sunk Island Review may buy their copies at £6.99, post-free. Cheques/P.O.s payable to Sunk Island Publishing. Publication date 28th September 1993. Copies can be ordered in advance.

paperback   180pp   ISBN 1 874778 10 8

SUNK ISLAND PUBLISHING
Sales Dept., P.O. Box 74
Lincoln LN1 1QG

HALLUCINATION OF AMERICA

José Hierro
translated by Louis Bourne

1.

Not rustling ears of grain
Over the rolling green, over the muttering, the panting
And the crack: it's a murmur
Soaking my life. (I found myself.
It lasted lightning's length. Again I was my own stranger.)
It was not a watery ear of wheat on my skin,
But a harvest of stars, light become wet shreds
Making me bright and unreal.
I crossed a frontier and something impossible
To understand happened.
It was as though sorrow's smoke
Soaked my unknown future.
I refused to find a name
For what fatally occurred.
I wanted to blind myself and disappear
In that powerful, free rhythm,
The ocean's swaying, the salty
Present, tireless movement erasing
Places, dates, deceptions, fervours, fears.
And what was sea I saw as a road.
As a road to the future. As fear.
As a noose of foam around my throat.

José Hierro

2.

Now I let myself rise and sink
Like a future corpse on the water.
If I lift my eyes, I see clouds and rocks.
From this side of the ocean I see them
As if I held them in memory
On the other side, there in that time.

My children play with the waves on the shore.
'Flap your wings, gulls, scream!'
They are here in America's waves.
One day we went off there to America.
I left my heart here on these shores,
My heart in the waters there,
Between these clouds and rocks I see now,
Remember, rather, lost for ever.

I went there with the sorrow of somebody closing
The chest holding the best things of his life.
I closed the golden lock with my failure,
And went there. Every day I kissed the wounds on my feet,
The marks of stones, thorns and brands.
I could cure them in America (the chemical industry's
Made unbelievable progress here on this shore):
I preferred to kiss them each day, lick them like a dog.
They tasted of Cordoba, Valencia, Salamanca and Barcelona,
Of the sea at Santander, the Madrid sierra, of fruit and wine,
The dust of roads, trains among oaks and agaves,
Of castles and cathedrals, taverns and prisons.

3.

It's this sea here that rocks my body.
For there – strange loyalty – I didn't go into the ocean.
My children told me: 'You did well
To bring us here, leaving that poor land behind...'
(That poor land, wrinkled, submissive,
Sunny, springlike, harsh and tender,
That bloodstained, flaking whitewash,
Lovely Spain, rich in holy oil, flowers and tears!)
They've lived there for some years (too many)
The children playing now in the waves.
They grew, worked, decided their life's course,
These children singing on the shore,
Not suspecting what happened, what has to.
'You did well,' they said, 'to leave that miserable land.'
(They've lived for some years without suspecting, beside
                                                  them,
There was an almost silent piece
Of that land they left on this side.)

4.

Not rustling ears of grain
Singing to me. Not stars, but sea pollen,
The light and murmur erasing all the music
Anchored in time, breathing that snuffs out
Every past and future word,
Turning us into eternal flame.

This blind seething – bless it! – blots out
An image occurring there, in America:

José Hierro

The agony of a man uttering words
In a language that's almost incomprehensible
To these children watching over him there,
These flapping now in the sun here.

Bless you, ocean. Behind your dazzling
Wall one cannot hear
The doctor there asking, 'What's he saying?'
It's these very waves, their murmur of life and death,
That will keep you from comprehending
These last words. And my secret will have returned
With me to the dark core of the land
That one day endured its weight.

VERTICAL POETRY 1

Roberto Juarroz
translated by Louis Bourne

Everything begins somewhere else.

It doesn't matter that some things
may still be here
and even end here:
here begins nothing.

That's why this word, this silence,
this table, the vase, your footsteps,
were never really here.

Everything's always somewhere else:
there where it begins.

VERTICAL POETRY 2

Roberto Juarroz
translated by Louis Bourne

There are days when air does not exist.
Miners of desolation,
we then breathe hidden substances.
And on the verge of choking,
we wander on with open mouths
and light no fires
so as not to use the little oxygen left
like a piece of yesterday's bread.

We no longer remember the names of our streets,
nor the size of our clothes,
the sound of our voices,
our bodies' sensation.

But all of a sudden,
as if they, too, had been left without air,
memory and forgetting drain away at the same time
and then we find
the tiniest possible density,
the wise particles where emptiness and life
touch.

And it's there, only there, we discover
salvation through the void.

NO PERFECTION

Mike Jenkins

Another new house
and still no perfection.

They should design them
as the Chinese did
with a fault built in:
so you search for one,
so when the roof falls in
it would be a bonus.

If you built a house
from the moon
then you'd dust
till you reached the foundations.

If you built it
from the sun
it could suffer
from spontaneous combustion.

A place of stars
could be constantly insisting
there was no protection.

So I invite them in
as guests for my house-warming:
the moon makes a crater

in the empty hearth,
the sun chars a pattern
over carpets and curtains
and stars blink subdued
disco-lights on ceilings.

I ask them all to leave
first thing in the morning.

FREESIAS

Janet Fisher

The valentine from the man she
eventually married said
what more do you want – blood?
but nothing from the man who'd taken her
to the ball, had brought her freesias
for her dress, had fingered her gently
in front of his gas fire as the man
she eventually married burst in
to borrow a match, and stood there.

THE SURVIVORS

Frans Pointl
translated by James Brockway

1987, Heemstede

I opened the little gate. The entrance to the back garden was shut off by an ugly wooden fence with a door in it.

The front-door was opened and a fat young girl of perhaps fourteen came walking towards me.

'You've come for the sunblinds?'

They must have advertised them. All at once I was acting the part of an interested customer. I nodded.

'They're back here, next to the shed. This way.' She opened the door in the fence.

The garden. No longer a wonderful wilderness – and where was the ivy? The pear-tree to the left, the apple-tree to the right. Sometimes, on earlier visits – clandestine visits – to the garden I'd stolen an apple or a pear. Fruit from a paradise I had lived in for eight years. Eating them had wrought no miracles.

I indicated the trees. 'Do they still bear fruit?'

'Yes, but not much.'

She pointed to a horribly unsightly shed which had swallowed up part of the lovely garden. 'Here are the sunblinds.'

Through the closed french windows I could see that the wall dividing the back-room from the kitchen had been demolished. They call that 'an open kitchen'. It almost made me angry to see it. Materially, the house belonged to someone else. Emotionally, it was still mine.

I passed my fingers over the faded orange linen as the girl began to babble about the size and the price.

'My parents aren't at home today,' she said.

'What a pity.' My role as a customer for the sunblinds might have gained me access to the interior of the house for a moment or two.

'Now you've seen them you could give us a ring tomorrow.' She went indoors and came back with a visiting card. *John W. Frost – Importer for Benelux of Durrell microwave ovens and washing-up machines.* 'My father's American,' she said proudly.

How had an American got it into his head to buy my home? I looked at the garden once more. A glass bell of quietude closed over me, dazing me. Familiar voices, scents, an innocence, a peace. For a moment a child stood there that bore my name.

1940, Heemstede

Every week-end I'm at home. It's no fun at that children's place. Grandpa, grandma and Aunty Henrietta, mother's youngest sister, are staying with us. Aunty Hetty looks like mother, but much younger.

Deck-chairs of red and white striped linen are standing in the garden. From the kitchen come wafts of matzoball soup. Grandpa is wearing a striped black suit with a broad white rubber collar. His tie is suspended from an elastic band. The tips of his white moustache curl upwards. He's walking about rattling tools. Mother's busy in the kitchen. The ivy has covered almost the whole of the side-wall with its shiny green leaves. Mother's got her long white dress on with a flowery apron over it. Aunty Hetty gets up out of her deck-chair and asks if she can help her.

The old piebald cat is chasing a butterfly and now and then leaps up in the air. The grass grows tall. Colourful flowers and green plants are dotted about here and there – it's all weeds.

The french windows are open too in our neighbours' house. A boy with black curly hair is playing a violin. Grandpa points at him and Aunty Hetty looks and listens. 'Elgar,' she says.

Grandma comes walking up. She walks with difficulty, leaning on a stick. She's wearing tall, brown, laced-up boots. Her left arm dangles down limply at her side, she drags her left leg, the foot is turned inwards. She stands still and looks at us. She smiles. Grandpa goes indoors and switches on the wireless, a big circular one of gleaming brown bakelite.

Spot, the cat, has caught a mouse. She keeps giving the tiny creature a rough tap. When the mouse tries to run away she's on it again with a great leap and flings it in the air with her extended claws. The little grey beast lies bleeding among the bushes.

'Grandma, grandma,' I cry. 'The cat will kill the mouse!'

Grandma comes, leaning on her stick, to look. 'That's nature,' she says.

Against the wall, close to the open french windows, stands the shining black piano. The brass arms for the candles gleam. New candles have been put in them. The lid is open. A purple runner lies over the keys. Perhaps mother will play later on.

The smell of flowers and food; familiar voices, a lukewarm wind. Every week-end I'm at home.

1945, Amsterdam

Of everything that she had possessed in the way of people and things, all that remained to her was: myself and the old Steinway piano.

I'm almost forgetting Uncle Simon, the doctor. It was as though he hadn't come back. We had last seen him in 1941, when he was staying with us in Heemstede with Aunty Annie and the plump twins, Simon and Nico. After the liberation he wrote to tell us he'd become a ship's doctor, had never much cared for the family and didn't feel like receiving visits for the time being. The letter had come from Athens. We still didn't yet know that his escapism had taken the form of drink.

Every time a letter arrived from the Red Cross, mother got out the photograph album. In the beginning I couldn't believe that we should never see grandpa and grandma, Aunty Hetty, Aunty Martha, Aunty Annie and the twins again. Perhaps it would have been a good thing if the piano had disappeared as well, it was so inextricably associated with french windows opening onto a fragrant garden and now lost forever. The big photograph album did disappear without trace later on.

Mother joined a group of Jewish spiritualists. The souls of the dead were floating and wafting about everywhere, she told me. At one of the séances they had told her that all her dead lived in the light and were happy.

I would often talk of Spot, our old cat, which we'd had to leave behind in all the haste. 'Poor Spot, I hope she is in the cat's heaven.'

'Animals do not go to heaven or into the light, because their souls are mortal,' mother informed me. 'That's why it is our duty to give them a heaven on earth.'

'Is that why people treat people the other way round?' I asked.

Uncle Solomon and Aunty Martha used to live in Beethoven Street. He imported fruit from the Mediterranean. Both their sons had been bosses at the market. By all sorts of roundabout routes mother had received a letter from uncle, from the assembly camp at Westerbork. In it he told her he had handed over diamonds, gold jewellery, silver serviette rings and damask to his upstairs neighbour, Gortjens, the police inspector, for safe-keeping.

In the beginning of October we sailed off in that direction.

On the hall stairs in Beethoven Street mother remarked that it was a strange experience to have to walk past Uncle Solomon's door.

Gortjens was in his sixties. He was big and broad. He held his head at a strange angle as though he looked down on everybody. I was struck by his strongly receding chin – or perhaps he had no chin. He had a big moustache which made it look as though his mouth were missing, too.

When mother was seated she looked carefully round the room. I saw Gortjens following her gaze.

'My brother and sister-in-law, who used to live downstairs, have not returned,' she said.

Gortjens said nothing. The door opened and a woman appeared. She was plump, fat, and had protruding eyes. Her head rested on an enormously thick neck. She had puffy little hands like a pig's trotters.

Mother spoke about the letter. Gortjens shrugged his shoulders, indifferent. He spread out his hands like a stall-keeper at the market.

'I have never received anything for safe-keeping. Can you see anything here, perhaps, that you recognize?'

'They'll be in the cupboards,' I thought.

My mother repeated the list of items in the letter, upon which Gortjens asked to see the letter.

'It's been lost.'

'Then you haven't a leg to stand on.' He lit a cigar and cast us an arrogant glance.

'Do you think my husband is lying?' Mrs Gortjens asked aggressively. During the conversation she had kept running one of her hands through her hair. I saw that her eyebrows were painted on – greasy little black stripes pointing upwards halfway up her plump forehead.

'If only you knew what I am thinking,' said my mother, getting up.

'That police inspector is as bad as the thieves he's supposed to catch,' she said as we walked down Beethoven Street.

All at once I noticed that I was alone. Mother had stopped outside a doorway and was reading the names on the board. I walked back.

'Mrs de Leeuw lived here. She's gone too.'

'Oh,' I said, for I hadn't known Mrs de Leeuw.

At times I felt blown up with death and emptied of life. I couldn't be carefree and happy like my classmates.

Frans Pointl

1946, Amsterdam

I was over thirteen, lean and small of stature. I'd had to stay down in the sixth class. At school they called after me with the name 'Sauerkraut'. I owed that to Martin van der Meer. He pestered me whenever he could and got others to do it too. I couldn't speak about it at home. Mother was withdrawing more and more into herself. At times I'd hardly get an answer to a question or anything I'd said. The tired folk who sometimes visited us recounted lists of names at which mother would nod. Dead, dead, they said. It echoed through me. Life seemed to consist purely of death.

I came out of school one Saturday morning. The sun was shining and I was walking, lost in thought, down Luta Street. Suddenly, at the corner of Tol Street, Martin and Theo van der Harst sprang out at me. I was no fighter and it was too late to run away. My satchel was knocked out of my hand and I was smacked to the ground. Laughing, Theo held fast to my wrists while Martin squatted across my chest and, with the triumph of a conqueror, lashed out at my face.

I arrived home with a bloody nose, a black eye and a cut lip. My clothes were knocked about too and this was what seemed to annoy mother the most. We hadn't the money to buy decent clothes. The social assistance gave us coupons. My measurements were taken by a woman who couldn't care less, in a big warehouse where they had only worn clothing. Old-fashioned striped trousers, far too baggy, jackets far too long, shirts that were too big for me, absurd pairs of shoes. I had charity to thank for making me walk around looking like a clown. Was this why they called 'Sauerkraut' after me?

Gerda, the timid Jewish girl from the fifth form, was there once, in the clothing warehouse. She blushed furiously when she saw me and looked quickly the other way. Later on, she told me that the nasty girls in her class called her 'vinegar'.

'Your clothes, they're all torn, for goodness sake,' was mother's reaction as she dabbed my lip and nose with a damp face-cloth and not too gentle a hand.

'Perhaps the assistance will find a nice old wedding-suit for me,' I said, mockingly.

Other boys had a father who could come to their assistance when something went wrong. I had no one. The idea of mother going to the teacher and complaining about Martin and Theo was unthinkable.

'Do I have to go to school on Monday?'

'Of course, you must. Are you afraid to? You must always stand up for yourself. If a person wants to get justice, he has to tackle the unpleasant things as well. We're going to The Hague next week, to that vicar where Henrietta worked, van Leden.'

I slept badly on Sunday night. I dreamed I flung Martin and Theo into a canal, but they got out and I had to flee. I woke up, dizzy, at halfpast six.

I arrived on the school playground far too early. No one was about. To my amazement Martin came strolling towards me. He fished an apple out of his pocket, took a bite at it and leaned on the wall of the gym hall, chewing. He saw me but ignored me.

It was as though I myself remained standing there and another boy stepped out of me. This other boy walked up to Martin and grabbed him roughly by the head so that the apple fell to the ground. The other boy slammed Martin's head hard against the wall. 'That's for last Saturday, two against one, eh, you dirty troublemaker. Slimy toad that you are. I bet you've got things at your home taken in for safe-keeping and never given back!'

When I let him go I saw to my surprise how he sagged soundlessly to the ground, his head again coming into contact with brick. A thick red stream flowed slowly across the murky paving stones. I turned round and walked home. I could never go to school again. It was only when I reached the spot where they'd given me a drubbing that Saturday that I began to shiver.

Arriving home, I found mother bent over the photograph album. Next to it lay a letter from the Red Cross. What she was now suffering was worse than what concerned me. She didn't seem to realize that I ought to be at school.

'Do you remember Aunty Tippy?' she asked.

I did. We'd paid her a visit in 'The Jewish Invalid' on Weesper Square at the beginning of the war. A dried-out little person as old as the hills. She kept asking mother: 'Who are you and who is that?' pointing to me.

I couldn't possibly believe the Germans would have dragged those terribly old people, already at death's door, out of the old people's home, shoved them into lorries and driven them to their deaths far from Amsterdam.

I pretended I had a headache and went to lie down on my bed. Mother, looking as though she were a waxen image, remained for a long time bent over the album.

After an hour had passed I decided to tell her what had happened. 'Excellent. An eye for an eye and a tooth for a tooth,' was her reaction but she added: 'And tomorrow back to school.'

That afternoon the bell went. Martin's furious parents came storming up the stairs.

'There's a big hole in our son's head and he's suffering from severe concussion. It's all your son's doing and we're going to the police *and* we're going to sue you!' they shouted.

For a moment I thought the father would attack me. Suddenly mother was standing in front of me with half a loaf in one hand and in the other the bread-knife, which she pointed at the infuriated parents. Her calm amazed me.

'Your son and another boy lay in wait for my son and then beat him up. Two against one, do you hear me? Do you see that black eye? That cut lip and nose? Perhaps it's at last been a lesson to your son. And now out of my house!'

She took a step forward and waved the bread-knife through the air, her dark eyes flashing.

Martin's parents retreated from the room.

'They forgot to gas you!' the woman shrieked from the stairs.

The matter had humiliating consequences for me. I was called to the headmaster's study and put on the mat. He told me I was abnormally aggressive and that I belonged to the Lombroso type, because my eyebrows met in the middle. He predicted that I was destined for the gallows. For a punishment I had to stand every day for three weeks from nine to ten in the morning under the big clock next to the school entrance.

I said nothing about that at home.

For a few weeks my mother was in a more approachable mood.

We went a walk along the river Amstel. Perhaps we might cross over on the ferry – it cost nothing.

She indicated the porter's lodge by the tram terminus and told me about the girl who had gone underground in the war but had walked about here so bravely. The hun in the lodge would always greet her in a servile manner. On one occasion he beckoned her over and offered her some German cake. Although she was almost dying of hunger, she'd refused.

At the café called 'Halfway to the Kalfje' a stately lady with grey hair passed us. She was dressed entirely in black. Mother came to a halt and looked round. She walked back and I followed. Coming to a stop before the old lady, she said, 'Aren't you Mrs Swaab? Don't you recognise me any more? Rebecca!'

'God in heaven, Rebecca, my child!' the old lady cried. They fell into each other's arms and kissed.

The old lady bore the marks of unsightly burns on her neck, chin and left cheek. She noticed mother's look of alarm and her hand in its black kid leather glove went up to her face.

'I can't speak to you about it and don't tell me what happened to you, either.'

'To think I should meet you again, Mrs. Swaab, I...'

She interrupted mother to say she wasn't called Swaab any more. Her name was now Mouton.

'You're married to a Mouton?'

'Oh, no, but I wanted to be rid of that Jewish name.'

Mother asked if she still played the piano, even if only for her pleasure. A touch of tragedy appeared on Mrs Mouton's face and she gazed past us with a sad look in her almost black eyes.

'My fingers will never touch the keys again.'

She asked me if I played the piano and as if I had no voice of my own, mother answered for me, saying I had no patience for that but was a fervent admirer of Liszt, Schubert and Mozart.

'Does he eat well?' Mrs Mouton asked, feeling my upper arm and shoulder with more strength that I would have credited her with.

'Nebbish, how bony he is. Get him some potatoes with tripe or gefilte fish – that makes men of them.' She stroked a hand across my hair. 'Isz doch mayn kind,' she said, putting a lot of sentiment into her voice.

She told us she lived in Menton and was sorry she would have no time over to visit us. She snapped her black bag open and fished a hundred guilder note out of it. 'Here you are, Rebecca. I'm sure you can do with it.'

Mother coloured up and gestured that she couldn't. 'I can't accept that,' she said.

'Don't make a fuss, child. Take it.' And she pushed the money into mother's hand and snapped her bag to. 'And now I must be getting on.' She gave mother a kiss and shook my hand.

We walked on further, a little embarrassed. Opposite the Zorgvlied cemetery we sat down on the side of the road and looked out over the water and quiet green fields.

In her day, Abigail Swaab had been a celebrated pianist, mother told me. She had given concerts in New York, Berlin, Warsaw, Moscow. She had been a friend of my grandma's. I thought it a strange idea that she had known mother as a schoolgirl.

'How old is Mrs Mouton?'

'She's in her eighties, but she's still got something of the grand touch about her that she used to have.'

I was amazed that someone could give away the enormous sum of a hundred guilders just like that, as though it were a mere box of matches.

Mother pointed out the Amstel Hotel. We heard the lapping of the water. 'A river like this goes flowing on, regardless,' mother muttered.

I thought about Mrs Mouton. She fascinated me.

'She wants to be rid of her Jewish name, yet she speaks Yiddish.'

'Who does?' mother asked, her mind elsewhere.

1946, The Hague

Aunty Hetty had worked for and lived in with a vicar in The Hague. When it was announced that the Jews had to report 'to be put to work in Germany' he had taken her to the camp at Vught himself.

In the train to The Hague mother sat staring out of the window, her face white. We had to take a tram from the main station to Valerius Street. *Ds. J.A. van Leder* it said on the shiny brass nameplate.

Mother rang. We waited. Shuffling footsteps and it was the vicar who opened the door.

'How do you do. I'd hardly have recognized you,' he said, with a puzzled little nod of the head. He went to shake her hand, but mother ignored it.

She replied to the effect that war made people unrecognizable.

As a boy of seven, I'd stayed a week with Aunty Hetty. I even remembered that the vicar slurped when he ate.

His head had grown leaner, the skin was stretched tight over his cheekbones. He'd kept his stiff little goatee beard.

Mother didn't go to the trouble of removing her coat. She sat down and started off straightaway.

'How could you throw her coolly into the lion's den like that? One who for so long and so loyally had seen to your housekeeping and bookkeeping for mere pocket-money and her keep! You did charitable work, rehabilitation of ex-prisoners. Mind my words, but not my deeds! The convicts you visit probably have a better record than you have. You could have married her, or found her an address where she could have gone underground!'

He blew his nose loudly and looked at me, scared. I stuck out my tongue, cheekily. He coughed and stroked his hand over his goatee. Mother walked to the door. 'It won't be long before you're a vicar no more! I'll see to that!'

Outside she expressed the opinion that the vicar and the policeman were bound to become good friends. War was a strange thing, she said, it brought out both the very best and the very worst in human beings.

1950, Haarlem

My Uncle Simon had gone downhill rapidly. He began to drink more and more. He'd been a ship's doctor for several shipping companies. Passengers on luxury cruise ships who needed his help were often confronted with a doctor who proved to be no longer fit to exercise his profession.

For a short time he succeeded in keeping off drink. He took up his residence again in his little villa on the edge of Haarlem. He applied for a post at a hospital in the town and got it. Six months later drink had got him in its grip again. He was dismissed. He lost his driving licence after he'd driven into a traffic sign-post, but, obstinately, he kept the damaged car, a Ford Prefect, 1947 model, parked outside his house.

I visited him now and then. After all, he was the only surviving relative we had.

'What shall I play for you?' He opened the lid of the piano, screwed up the piano stool a bit and took his seat. Aunty Annie's photo with the twins, Nico and Simon, stood on the piano. Their plump child's arms and legs swelled out of their sailor's suits. Uncle never mentioned them.

'I asked you a question.' He turned round towards me.

I looked at his eyelids which were like pink shells. There was a melancholy but at the same time mocking look in his dark-brown eyes.

'Scriabin.'

He sat for a moment or two lost in thought, his slender hands held motionless above the keys. Then he conjured a kaleidoscopic waterfall of sound out of them. Mesmerized, I allowed myself to be seduced by lyricism, a pianistic hammering, sadness and sheer driving power.

There was a sharp ring on the bell. He interrupted his playing and got up.

'Doctor, quickly! My husband has had another heart attack. The capsule under his tongue hasn't helped, he can't get any air into his lungs!'

'So, so,' said uncle.

I knew he didn't care for the Zootjes family owing to their unpatriotic attitude during the war. The man had been a prominent Dutch Nazi and had been in prison for it. Uncle ignored them.

We got into the neighbours' garden through uncle's neglected one. Sideways, in a low chair, lay a fat, bald man with his hand pressed to his neck. His lips were purple, his eyes were popping. A noise was coming out of his throat which reminded me of my fretsaw.

Uncle took hold of the man's arm and counted his pulse while looking at his watch. I stared at uncle's arm, at the number tattooed onto it in a dark pigment with a circle drawn roughly round it.

'Do something, do!' his neighbour's wife implored him. The over-abundant and badly smoothed-out rouge on her broad cheek-bones gave her a feverish look.

'One moment.' Uncle stood up.

'Quickly, quickly!' she cried. I saw her enormous breasts trembling.

He was back in a moment, a syringe in his one hand, a stethoscope in the other. He stuck the needle into Mr Zootjes upper arm and emptied the syringe into it. Thirty seconds later, the sawing noise came to an end. The mouth puffed out air. As though he were blowing out a candle on a birthday cake, I thought.

Uncle remained crouched at his side, watching the face with eager intensity, the face in which the motionless eyes stared up into the blue. Putting the stethoscope to his ears and opening Zootjes' shirt, uncle placed the other end of the instrument on the man's chest. He listened intently, every now and then moving the stethoscope an inch or two.

Mrs Zootjes stood looking on and wringing her hands.

1951, Haarlem

When I visited uncle again I decided to get a clear answer to a question that had been bothering me for a year.

We were drinking coffee in the kitchen.

'Is Mrs Zootjes still living there?' I began. A superfluous question, for I'd seen her copious form behind the net curtains as I'd passed.

'Yes, and more dolled up than ever.' He took a sip at his coffee.

'When he got that heart attack last year, you helped him into the next world, didn't you?' I kept my eyes fixed on him but he didn't even blink. A saucy expression appeared on his face and a slow smile formed round his lips.

'A matter of neighbourly duty.'

He got up energetically and walked into the living-room. Taking his place at the piano on which a bottle of whisky was standing, he unscrewed the cap and took a gulp.

Then he turned round towards me, stretched his fingers a few times and asked: 'Rachmaninoff, Scriabin, Liszt or Schubert?'

SHADES OF MONK

Nicholas Royle

A day out was a big event and my mother never quite left enough time to be ready in time for when my father had said we should leave. As the hour approached he would march around the lounge and dining room, his footfalls becoming heavier as the minute hand crawled round the clock. Then he would stomp upstairs, his face like granite, and shout: 'Do you know what the time is?'

Invariably my mother answered, 'I'm ready,' when she clearly wasn't. He could see she nearly was but instead of waiting patiently he stormed into the lounge, slamming the door after him so that the whole house shook. He would put on a record and pour himself a whisky. He made sure to play something he knew my mother particularly disliked. His jazz collection ranged from the earliest to the most avant garde, and when he wanted to upset her he would put on something modern. She could listen to trad jazz and singers like Billie Holiday and Sarah Vaughan, but anyone later than early bebop left her cold. She would *put up* with almost anything, of course, to avoid rows, because she knew how much they upset me. I suffered from asthma, induced by stress.

To upset her he would select the Modern Jazz Quartet or Sonny Rollins or Thelonious Monk and play it at such volume that everything vibrated. The noise seemed to penetrate the grain of the wood that held the house together. Sometimes now I wonder if he didn't contrive arguments just to give himself an opportunity to listen to the records my mum didn't like.

If I was unlucky enough to be caught in the lounge when he slammed the door I would be trapped there, unable to get up and leave for fear of enraging him further. But his behaviour in these circumstances had become fairly predictable and I would normally creep out of the lounge as soon as I heard him coming downstairs.

After some time my mother appeared, trailing a thick cloud of Chanel No 5 which my father got for her cheap somewhere, perhaps because he thought she ought to have the best, or maybe because he'd once saved and bought it for her years ago, and meant it. To me that perfume came to be associated with tension and an overbearing feeling of suffocation.

She pretended there was nothing the matter and told me to get my coat and follow her out to the car. I dragged my feet through the garage, momentarily gripping the handlebars of my bike and wishing I could just get on it and go off somewhere by myself. I'd get to the car and climb in the back. It was a dark green Mark II Jaguar, registration 330 CNY, with lots of lovely chrome at the front and distinctive wire-spoked wheels. The dash was polished wood and the upholstery rich, brown leather. I felt sick, though, almost as soon as I got in because of the combination of smells: petrol, leather and Chanel No 5. In the passenger seat my mother would have bent the rearview mirror round so she could apply her lipstick, then she would put it back and of course it was impossible to get it in exactly the right place. She would close her lips down on a tissue, then without looking round she would ask me if I was looking forward to the trip. She spoke briskly and cheerfully as if nothing was wrong. I answered in monosyllables because I was worried about the row and couldn't focus my mind on anything else.

'What if he doesn't come out?' I asked her.

'He'll come,' she replied.

And he always did, after about ten minutes, looking like thunder and smelling of drink. If anything annoyed my mum more than Thelonious Monk it was alcohol. She had good reason to fear it: when my father drank, his temper deteriorated and he sometimes turned violent. I remember vividly the time he belted her and began tearing her dresses to shreds and throwing them out of the bedroom window on to the back lawn. She beat her fists on the grass while I crouched behind my toy cupboard quietly asphyxiating.

To reverse out of the drive my father would look in the rearview mirror and have to straighten it. Every time I was terrified he would realise it was my mother who had moved it, but he never picked up on this.

When he'd had a drink he drove faster and used the horn frequently, swearing at anyone who got in his way. Once in Chester a policeman was directing traffic the wrong way and causing unnecessary delays, and my father leaned out of his window and called the policeman a twat. On reflection it's one of the few things I admire him for. At the time I didn't know what the word meant but the look my mum gave him indicated its flavour. Because they weren't rowing I was excited. Generally, though, my father's swearing was in the context of a row and he drove so fast and erratically that my mother had to grip the strap above her window and she would turn, white-faced, and glare at him. In the back I cowered, tracing the cracks in the leather seat with my finger.

On our arrival at Buxton or Chapel-en-le-Frith one of two things would happen. Either my father would get out of the car and march off expecting us to follow, or he would park the car and simply sit in the driving seat staring off into space with his face quite set. In the second event my mother would wait a short while then say something like, 'Come on, Andrew, let's be making a move.' My father's only reaction would be to sniff and if I looked closely I could see the lines around his mouth deepen slightly. I would open the car door gingerly and close it behind me as if the car were packed full of delicate china.

'Where are we going?' I would ask my mother as she took my hand. 'What about ... him?' I couldn't bring myself to call him Dad when things had reached such a state. Depending on how serious the row was my mother would either respond, 'Oh he's all right. He'll come round,' or she would show her true feelings: 'Your father can sit and rot for all I care.' I had noticed how they both distanced themselves from each other. When things were OK between them he was 'your dad' and she was 'your mam', but at bad times they became 'your father' and 'your mother'. I used to gauge the seriousness of a row by how one referred to the other and I was always terrified by any sentence beginning 'Your mother...'

What usually happened was he would march off and we would try and catch up with him, but as soon as we did he would put on another spurt. This was how I saw many places for the first time.

It might have been Buxton or Chapel, I didn't know which, but one of them was laid out before me in lights. It was a dark night and my geography always was very parochial: I knew all the short cuts to the nearest railway junction and the best stretch of the canal. It got no better as I got older and I came to understand London in terms of the lines drawn between my home, my girlfriend's flat, my office and my favourite pubs and restaurants.

I was parked at the top of a hill in the Peak District looking north and somewhere in that cosmos of neon was the centre of either Buxton or Chapel.

Nicholas Royle

It was at least twenty years since I had seen either town.

I had decided to spend Christmas driving round the Peaks in the Mini. I'd rented a cottage for a few days but was expected in Wythenshawe at some point. My mother and father still lived there in the same house.

I started to shiver and pulled my collar up. Walking back to the car I saw drizzle dancing in the headlamps like clouds of midges. The Mark II Jag was still easily the best-looking car on the road, but beyond my means. In many ways the Mini was ideal. It looked good, sounded good, drove well and was cheap to run. It would more than do until I could afford a Jag.

It had its drawbacks – I started the engine – the noise being one of them. Out of all the tapes I'd got stacked up in the map pockets the only one I could hear over the noise of the engine when I was going fast was a Thelonious Monk tape my father had recorded and sent me as an early Christmas present. Since I do like to travel fast I'd been listening to this over and over again. There was something about the depth and weight of the sound of the tenor sax, drums, bass and piano that allowed the music to be heard over the noise of the engine.

My father being my father, he had written out in full on the cassette inlay card all the details of the recording: song titles, personnel, writing credits, date and place and performance. I was slightly disturbed to observe when I first examined these notes that the original recording was made on May 21, 1963 at a concert in Tokyo. The other side of the world from Wythenshawe but only two months and one day after the day I was born. I didn't think that would be the reason for my father sending it to me, but it struck me as strange. He sent me tapes every so often and I would write and say thank you, parcelling up jazz magazines I picked up for him free in London. I always listened to the tape at least once or twice but this Monk tape had got into my head in a way no other had. It may have been partly the association with the past or it may just have been the music itself. They do say he was a genius.

At first it sounded raucous and impenetrable. I could see why it didn't appeal to my mum and, to be honest, as a child I could neither understand the music my father played, nor distinguish one artist from another. Apart from one or two unusual singers like Blossom Dearie and Billie Holiday it all sounded the same. And because it was all we ever got to hear – unless I felt brave enough to ask if we could listen to the Top 40 on a Sunday evening – I grew antagonistic towards it. It took a long time to grow out of that and realise that during those years it was in fact seeping into me and I'm now as big a fan as my father used to be. In recent years he's been selling off his record collection and I've built up a stock of CDs. He was selling what he never listened to, ostensibly so he could buy CDs instead, but I suspected from his general attitude that he was winding down for the end. Knowing my father has given me an opportunity to observe depression at work, to watch the way it ate him away from the inside like a parasite.

I turned the car round and headed back through the rain to the cottage. Leaving the main road I had to negotiate a single track road for a mile, then cross a sheep grid and turn into a rough track with thick clumps of grass growing up the middle. My little car bumped along resolutely and I got nervous when I thought I could smell something burning and couldn't imagine what it might be. The music got louder. The smell persisted until the tape clicked off, then it seemed to disperse. I wondered if the stereo was overheating, or was there something outside in the fields?

I flipped the tape over and changed down to first for the final, steep ascent into the yard in front of the cottage. I could hear the grass in the middle of the track scraping harmlessly on the underside and I saw now why the owner wanted to make sure when I spoke to her on the phone that I didn't drive a three-wheeler. 'We had someone once who drove this funny little car, Reliant Robin,' she said to me. 'Oh it was funny. Shouldn't laugh, but he had to walk the last half mile.' Not wishing to appear rude, I had laughed along with her as if I'd got the joke, which I hadn't, but I did now.

Monk continued to play after I switched off the engine. I took the key out of the ignition and still the music played. I felt sure that since I'd switched off the electrics the stereo should stop working and couldn't remember whether a similar thing had happened before. I wondered if it might be possible for the stereo to be wired direct to the battery and therefore operable without the ignition. After all, the headlamps could be switched on and off without the key. I pressed the switch and flooded the rainswept cottage in yellowish light to prove it to myself. The music still played and the burning smell had returned. It reminded me more than anything of a lit cigar.

I went into the cottage, undressed in the dark and got straight into bed. I fell asleep almost instantly and in the early hours dreamt I heard voices murmuring outside. They shone a yellow light over the windows and I wondered dimly who was stealing my car and why they were foolish enough to switch the lights on. All the time the Monk tape was going round and round in my mind.

While I was drifting in and out of sleep just before dawn I had a bizarre series of thoughts about the Peak District, most of which fled like wisps of dreams as soon as I came properly awake. But some remained and their main thrust seemed to be that the Peaks was not an ordinary place. Because it was so much a part of my childhood memories and mythology it was set apart from the rest of the world. Anything could happen here and it would be as real as the events and scenes I remembered.

The further I came out of sleep the less sense these ideas made, but I knew they had seemed so logical to my dozing mind.

The Peaks had become part of my imaginary world because of the links I had with the region as a child and because of the twenty-year gap between then and now.

Weak light filtered through the skylights and dispersed my rambling thoughts. I reached for my watch and saw it was early. As I reached for my clothes I realised with distaste that they smelt of smoke, as if I'd spent the evening in a pub. There was a clean T-shirt in my bag. Collecting the map from beside the bed, I went to fix some breakfast and it was the festive silver top on the milk bottle that reminded me it was Christmas Day.

I wasn't unhappy to be spending Christmas alone for the first time. Sara had gone to her parents' and, of course, I was intending to drop in on mine.

I had planned to drive close to Kinder Scout and do some walking, so I took the A625 out of Chapel past Rushup Edge and towards the enigmatic shimmering giant of Mam Tor. It was a beautiful day, bright and fresh, and for some reason the Monk complemented the conditions. In fact, with the window open it was quite chilly, so I closed it and only then realised why I had opened it in the first place: the car had reeked of stale cigar smoke and the windows had been misted up.

I dropped down into Winnats Pass and drove through the Hope Valley, turning left on to the A6013 to Ladybower Reservoir. There I picked up the A57 westbound and motored uphill alongside the River Ashop. The names were all distantly, achingly familiar to me. After about six miles I pulled over and got out. The air was moist here. I had parked at the beginning of a stretch of woodland. As I pulled on my hiking boots and laced them up I thought how I was repeating the actions of a hundred hiking trips taken with my father: sitting with the car door open, half in and half out, anticipating the walk ahead, and listening to Thelonious Monk.

Only this time I was in control. There was only me, no longer a pawn in my father's power struggle. We often used to go hiking together, the two of us, partly because my mum wasn't that keen and partly because if he got me on his own he could score points. If things were going well between him and my mum, that's all he did, score points. But if they had been rowing, a day out with me in the Peaks gave him the opportunity, firstly, to try and turn me against my mum ('your Mother'), and, secondly, to attempt to get round me.

He failed in these as in most things, but I don't think he was aware of it. For myself I was walking a tightrope between loyalty to my mum and the fear of him turning against me.

Once, when we'd parked the car in Edale, he was still white with anger from a row they'd had that morning and he just marched off into the hills. I had to run to catch up then trot several yards behind him, pretending to be engrossed in the action of walking. I didn't dare go any closer to him, but neither could I lag behind too much. These rules had never been articulated. I had intuited them myself over the years. After a mile or two he'd stop, drop the rucksack and get out the packed lunch my mum had prepared and always would whatever the circumstances. She would never let him have the chance to accuse her of not correctly performing her duties. In the course of their screaming matches he would invariably yell at some point, 'I'm the one who goes out to work in this house. I'm the one who pays the bills.' I realised at an early age that paying the bills gave you the right to torment and abuse those around you.

I crossed the road and dived into the wood. On the other side of the trees was a flat area of long grass leading to the slopes of Kinder Scout. I started to climb up the path alongside Fair Brook. It was mid-afternoon and the sky had clouded over but there was no mist. I reckoned it was safe. The slope steepened and I had to pick my way between large rocks and clumps of spongy grass. Soon I stopped and looked back. I was already quite high up and could not make out the car. In fact, I couldn't see the road, but the wood was my landmark.

I was hungry and wished I had one of my mum's packed lunches: tuna sandwiches on brown bread wrapped up in silver foil, a boiled egg and a tomato wrapped separately, and a Kitkat or a Viscount Cream.

Looking back up the mountain I realised I should get a move on. The clouds seemed much closer now than before. The brook trickled innocently on my left. At some point before the waterfall I would have to cross it. I put my head down and concentrated on covering ground. My breathing was regular and healthy. As a child I would be panting at this stage and wheezing with asthma, but I knew I had to keep up. Ample opportunity was afforded me to study him from the back. In particular I examined the back of his head and neck, wondering where the softest spot might be in case I ever had to kill him to protect my mum. There were plenty of weapons: brass candlesticks, the poker, knives, hammers and wrenches.

One thing that terrified me when they were going at each other was the thought that my mum might kill him and be locked away, or that she would try and he would overpower her. I knew he was clever enough at twisting words to defend himself successfully if he killed her. And then I'd be alone with him.

The top of Kinder Scout is a plateau of about five or six square miles dotted with cairns and trig points. I pulled my body over the last outcrop and stood up. I breathed deeply and gave a long, satisfied sigh. I looked down and could just make out the wood. I knew I would have to head down almost immediately since the hour was getting late. But I had time to wander a little way. I felt as if I was standing on the edge of a vast wonderland and it would be a terrible shame not to have just a little look before departing.

I was stupid, very stupid. For all his faults my father would not have been so foolish. Within minutes I was surrounded by mist or cloud. I told myself it was cloud as if that mitigated my stupidity, but it made no difference: I was lost.

I walked slowly for fear of stepping over the edge of the plateau. When the mist cleared I thanked God, then cursed myself when it wrapped its cloak around me once more. I recalled a piece of advice that one should remain still and wait for the mist to clear. But if I waited it would be dark and then I'd never get down alive.

What would my father have done? He would surely have found a way through the mist. I was just wandering round in circles getting myself hopelessly lost. I began to feel panic rising inside me. Hot tears pricked my eyes. My chest tightened and my breathing became fast and shallow. I was scared that either way – whether I fell over the edge or was stranded on the mountain all night – I would die.

My footfalls were flat and dull. I was getting rapidly colder as my clothes soaked up the moisture. The smell of damp wool and cotton sparked off a poignant memory of unloading my mother's washing machine and helping her hang things out on the line, passing her the pegs so she wouldn't have to hold them in her mouth. I didn't have a washing machine myself and all you could smell at the launderette was cigarette smoke.

I carried on even though my hopes were fading fast. After a while I convinced myself there was a dark shadow ahead of me in the mist and I followed it, recognising the hunched shoulders and bristling neck of my father in one of his blackest moods.

I didn't realise it at the time but my father was more childish than I was. We sometimes used to have mock fights in which I could hit as hard as I liked and if it ever looked like I was winning he would tell me off for being too aggressive, then sulk for the rest of the day.

Sometimes he did hit me. When I was thirteen or so he stirred his tea and touched the back of my hand with the hot spoon, making me flinch with pain. 'Christ,' I snapped. 'That was stupid.' He dealt me a stinging blow across the face and told me never to swear at him again. 'Get upstairs,' he ordered. My mum started to stick up for me – 'Oh Brian, he didn't mean it' – but I was already half out of the door. As I climbed the stairs I heard his voice rise like a wasp and I knew my mum was about to get stung for me once again.

So when I saw him up there on Kinder in the mist I followed him as I always had. Too frightened to disobey, too much in awe of him to show disrespect, too scared to act on my own initiative, I had lived all my life in his shadow.

We passed a boulder slewed awkwardly on its side. Had we passed it before? Were we going round in circles? After some time we passed it again. Was it a trick of the mist? A boulder that looked the same? My father didn't stop so it was best to keep following. He would know where we were headed and if we were going round in circles there would be a reason for it.

The hunch of his shoulders was a warning not to get too close and not to lag too far behind. I was walking among fist-sized rocks. It would be so easy to pick one up and land a fatal blow on the back of his head. I would be freeing my mother, myself, and him also from his depression.

We passed the rock again but from a different angle and I realised suddenly what was happening: we were following a figure of eight, the infinity symbol. I felt a wave of sadness wash over me. The man was a prisoner, his own prisoner and his own gaoler, trapped in a self-fulfilling prophecy. Not for the first time I felt sorry for him.

Then I smelt something other than the damp smell of defeat. Penetrating the nimbus around me came the unmistakable scent of cigar smoke. I faltered and the shadow ahead of me increased its lead. I sniffed at the smoke and lunged forward for my father at the same time. But he had gone. I had let him go.

I followed the cigar smoke away from the infinite path of my father's madness and soon heard music drifting through the translucent air. Each note hung in the mist, both cleansed and numbed by the moisture, but it was clearly recognisable as *Bemsha Swing*. The louder the music became, the faster I walked, the more pungently burnt the cigar, and within a short time I was at the edge. I glimpsed another shadow standing by the edge of the waterfall, but knew it wasn't my father. I told myself it was just a rock and started picking my way precariously down the slope. As I descended the mist thinned and I could see twenty yards in front of me, then fifty. But so much time had elapsed on the mountain that it was fast getting dark. I calculated I had long enough to reach the car. The smell of smoke had dissipated as I ploughed through clumps of wet grass and sprigs of heather and kicked up clods of sodden earth. I heard nothing other than the skidding of my boots and the rasping of my chest.

The air was clear enough now for me to see as far as the strip of woodland but night's curtain had fallen and I had to trust my sense of direction once I left the side of Fair Brook. When I plunged into the wood it was too dark even to see where I was placing my feet and I began to panic in case I lost my way so close to the end. But I didn't need to worry because I could hear music again: *Straight, No Chaser* winding its way between the boles of the densely packed fir trees. The effect was as if someone were standing by the car poking a torch beam into the wood. Indeed, as I neared the road I could see the car glowing like a beacon, yet I had surely left the interior lights off. Had I not they would have drained the battery in the time I'd been gone and would scarcely still be as bright as they were now. In fact, they were burning so brightly they all but eclipsed the four silhouettes sitting in the car, three in the back and one in the passenger seat.

Thelonious Monk, piano. Charlie Rouse, tenor saxophone. Butch Warren, bass. Frankie Dunlop, drums. The five of us drove back to the cottage. They didn't let up once on the journey. *Just a Gigolo, Evidence, Jackie-ing*. Everyone had room but I wasn't exactly in a position to pick up hitch-hikers. I had to open the window to disperse the smoke, and Warren, who was breathing down my ear, stank of alcohol. I made a mental note not to allow him near the controls of the car. I took the speed up to 80 on the A6 between Chapel and Dove Holes but could still hear every phrase. I could hear Warren's finger pads scraping down the strings of his bass and the click of the keys on Rouse's sax as clearly as the music itself.

Although there was plenty of room in the cottage and I had no objection to them coming in, the quartet preferred to stay in the car overnight. I fell asleep to the impudent staccato phrasing of *Bemsha Swing* and woke, unaware of having dreamt, to *Pannonica* three songs later on the tape. I didn't know how many times they went through the other tracks, but I was glad the cottage was in an isolated location.

As soon as I was fully awake I knew I couldn't put it off any longer. I had a quick breakfast and joined the band in the car. Half an hour up the A6 and we were in Stockport, from where it was only a few minutes to Wythenshawe. As I turned into Biddall Drive my heart was pounding. The windows were wound up but Minis are thin-skinned little cars and I was worried about disturbing the neighbours on Boxing Day morning. I pulled into my parents' drive and cut the engine as the car rolled under the shelter of the carport. My father's car would have been in the pink garage at the back of the house.

They didn't seem surprised to see me. 'We were expecting you,' my mum said. I kissed her. My father stretched a smile across his miserable features and shook my hand. I was anxious to get into the lounge and change the music from Sarah Vaughan, which wouldn't mask the sound I could hear quite clearly coming from the car outside, to Thelonious Monk.

'Do you mind?' I asked as I ejected the CD and slipped Tokyo Concerts Vol 1 from its case. My father's face was slipping back to normal and I saw a shadow darken my mother's brow for an instant. But I felt happier when the Monk was playing. My father sat down in his chair and pressed his finger against the side of his nose. A hypochondriac all his life he'd obviously found a new ailment. My mum disappeared into the kitchen to start lunch. I wondered about sneaking something out to the musicians but realised how silly that was: they were managing perfectly well without me.

'Is that your car out there?' my mum called. I rushed into the kitchen. She was craning her neck to see out of the window in the back door.

I nodded briefly and caught her hands to pull her round. 'You're looking good,' I said.

'I'm not,' she answered, busying herself at the sink.

I mouthed to her: 'How's *he*?'

I thought that if I avoided calling him Dad it would make my mum realise how I wasn't close to him, because I always feared she thought we were good friends.

She raised her eyebrows and rolled her eyes and whispered, 'Terrible.' She looked over my shoulder to make sure he wasn't in the doorway. 'He's got something wrong with his nose.'

'I know,' I said. 'I saw him pressing it.'

She tutted, then asked, 'Do *you* like this music?'

'It's all right,' I said, feeling awful. 'I'd better go back in.' I always had to be careful not to spend too much time alone with my mum or else he would assume we were talking about him and start sulking.

I went and sat with him and he asked me a few questions about my work although he wasn't in the slightest bit interested. I told him I'd been up Kinder Scout the day before and he just snorted, betraying no sign that he'd been up there too. At lunch he slouched in his chair and pushed his food around his plate with his fork in his right hand, pressing his nose flat with his other hand. Whenever I went home my mum would cook something a little different. My father peered at his rice as if it were a mass of maggots.

'Your father doesn't like anything different,' my mum announced. I nodded almost imperceptibly.

The CD finished. And started again. I had put it on repeat. My mother looked unhappy. We somehow got through lunch and I said I was going to call round and see Dave Entwistle, an old friend from school. I had no intention of seeing him and interrupting his holiday, but the excuse got me out of the house for the afternoon. I drove around the neighbourhoods I used to play in as a child, past the gravel path where Alex Morgan fell and skinned his thumb and knees, around the top of the rec where we played football, past the carpark where I once stole the Ford badge off a Ford Escort. I bounced over the humpback bridge at Skelton Junction and kept pace with the canal for a few hundred yards. I had to keep the windows wound up because of the noise.

As soon as I walked back in the house I thought of something else. 'Dave's dad was there,' I improvised, 'smoking cigars.' I had to explain the smell or they would ask. My mum said she couldn't smell anything though I didn't know how. 'Your father's gone to bed,' she told me. I was relieved. I helped her prepare some tea for both of us. As I watched her slicing cucumber I was seized by the fear that she might cut herself. 'Be careful with that,' I said. She told me not to be so silly. Then I became aware of the music from outside the kitchen door. I had to put the CD on again so my mum wouldn't hear it. If she knew they were out there she'd have to ask them in even though unexpected guests were a bother. If my father knew they were out in the car he'd ask them in just to annoy her. I hated doing it but I had to, and it had to be Monk.

My mum wanted to eat in the kitchen but I persuaded her to come into the lounge and sit on the settee. She told me how a few days ago they had been in a lite-bite in town and he had called her a fucking twat loud enough for everyone to hear. She had wanted the ground to open and swallow her up.

'He threatened to walk out the other day,' she said. 'Started getting his suitcase out of the loft, saying he'd effing had enough and was going.'

'Well, what happened?' I asked. 'Why's he still here?'

'He can't just walk out like that, you know.' My mum showed me the yellowing bruises on her wrists. 'That's where my hands got knocked against the stepladder trying to shove his suitcase back into the loft.'

'Why didn't you let him go?' I asked in complete bafflement.

She looked at me as if I was stupid. 'You wouldn't understand,' she said. 'You're too much like him.'

It always hurt me whenever she said that. The music was obviously upsetting her but I couldn't turn it off because then she'd hear it coming from outside. I looked at her hurt face and desperately wanted to tell her how much I loved her and how bad I felt about how much she had had to put up with from him in order to protect me.

'I love you,' I said but she couldn't hear me over the applause for Frank Dunlop's drum solo in *Straight, No Chaser*.

I waited until my mum went to bed then lay down on the settee. The music was still on but I'd turned down the volume so that now there was a slight echo effect coming from outside. I lay there puzzling over why she hadn't let him go when he was about to. So many times in the past she had said she couldn't wait for an opportunity to leave him, which I knew wouldn't arise at least until I had left home. So when he was offering to go, why didn't she let him?

It disturbed me to think that perhaps she had become so accustomed to his abuse she now depended on it. Maybe she'd been trapped for so long the idea of freedom scared her.

In the early hours I slipped out of the house and set off back to London. I left Monk and the other musicians behind at Knutsford services on the M6 by persuading them to get out and stretch their legs.

CONTRIBUTORS

JUDI BENSON is an American poet and artist living in London. She is the editor of Foolscap magazine. Her first collection of poems, Somewhere Else, was published by Turret Books in 1991. Another collection is due from Rockingham Press.

LOUIS BOURNE has lived in Spain for the last twenty-five years and is studying for a PhD. As well as his own poems his translations of Spanish poets have appeared in many magazines and anthologies including *New Directions 30, Granite, Stand, International Poetry Review* and *Outposts*. His most recent book is *Contemporary Poetry from the Canary Islands* (Forest Books), edited by Sebastián Nuez Caballero.

JAMES BROCKWAY has been publishing his translations of Dutch literature since 1947. He received the Martinus Nijhoffprijs for his services to Dutch literature in 1966. His poems, short stories and translations have appeared in *Iron, Stand, London Magazine* and many other magazines. Enitharmon recently published a book-length collection of his translations of Rutger Kopland, *A World Beyond Myself*. His account of living in Holland, 'Over There on a Visit', appeared in our last issue.

MATTHEW CALEY lives in London and is a graphic designer. His poems have appeared in many magazines. Collections of his poetry include *Hicks* (Echo Room Press, 1986), and *Protacool* (Wide Skirt Press, 1987).

JOHN CAYLEY is a poet and translator as well as the publisher of Wellsweep Press. His work has appeared in numerous magazines and books, including *Looking Out From Death: the new Chinese poetry of Duo Duo* (Bloomsbury, 1989), and *Gu Cheng, an authorized translation* (Renditions: Hong Kong, 1990).

JANET FISHER lives near Huddersfield, where she is a co-director of The Poetry Business. Her third collection of poems, *Nobody Move* is published by Slow Dancer.

STEPHEN GREGORY's first novel, *The Cormorant* (Heinemann, 1986) won the Somerset Maugham Award and a prize from the Welsh Arts Council. It has also been televised. Another novel, *The Woodwitch*, followed in 1988. Stephen Gregory's stories have been published in a number of magazines in the UK and abroad.

JOSÉ HIERRO was born in Madrid in 1992. He was imprisoned for over four years at the age of seventeen, accused of helping civil war prisoners. He was a founding editor of the poetry magazine *Proel*. He has published eight books, including *Libro de las alucinaciones* (*Book of Hallucinations*, 1964) and *Agenda* (1991). He has received the Adonais, National, Critics' and Principe de Asturias Prizes.

MIKE JENKINS teaches in a comprehensive school in Merthyr Tydfil. His latest book of poems, *A Dissident Voice*, was published by Seren Books.

Contributors

PHILIP SYDNEY JENNINGS has had many stories published in magazines and anthologies, including *Iron, Panurge* and *The Pan Book of Horror Stories*. He tutors Creative Writing at the City Literary Institute in London and has an MA in Creative Writing from City College, New York.

WANG JIAXIN was born in 1957 in Hubei Province, China and graduated from Wuhan University in 1982. He served as an editor of *Poetry Magazine* in Beijing and was co-editor of a number of anthologies. He has published three collections of poetry. Since falling out of faviour with the authorities in 1989 he has been deprived of employment in China and now lives in Europe.

ROBERTO JUARROZ's first collection of poems, *Vertical Poetry*, appeared in Buenos Aires in 1958. Further volumes with the same title successively numbered have been published over the years. He edited the Argentinian literary magazine, *Poesia-Poesia* from 1958 to 1965 and was awarded the Grand Prize of the Argentine Poetry Foundation in 1977.

FRANS POINTL is one of Holland's best-known authors.

NICHOLAS ROYLE is a chief sub-editor on a national weekly magazine in London. His stories have appeared in numerous magazines and anthologies, including *Fiction Magazine, Interzone* and *Reader's Digest*. He edited *Darklands*, an anthology of psychological horror stories, published by Egerton Press in 1991.

PETER RYDE grew up in London, but has lived in south Lincolnshire since 1960. His first ambition was to run a snack bar; his second was to be a novelist. Instead, he became a teacher, technical journalist and film producer. Now retired, he works part-time as a film archivist. During the last eight years his poems and stories have appeared in a number of magazines and anthologies.

ANNIE WRIGHT lives in Scorton, near Richmond, Yorkshire.